D0743569

CALGARY PUBLIC LIBRARY

JUL ☐ ☐ 2007.

THE GIRL
ON THE
VIA FLAMINIA

Also by

ALFRED HAYES

The Shadow of Heaven

All Thy Conquests

The Big Time

In Love

My Face for the World See

Alfred Hayes

THE GIRL ON THE VIA FLAMINIA

With an Introduction by
Paul Bailey

Europa
editions

Europa Editions
116 East 16th Street
New York, N.Y. 10003
www.europaeditions.com
info@europaeditions.com

This book is a work of fiction. Any references to historical events,
real people, or real locales are used fictitiously

Copyright © 1949 by Alfred Hayes
First Publication 2007 by Europa Editions

All rights reserved, including the right of reproduction
in whole or in part in any form

"Chronicles of Dust and Sin" by Paul Bailey first appeared in
The Guardian, on 29, October 2005
It is reprinted in this publication with kind permission from the author,
©2005 Paul Bailey

Library of Congress Cataloging in Publication Data is available
ISBN-13: 978-1-933372-24-2
ISBN-10: 1-933372-24-9

Hayes, Alfred
The Girl on the Via Flaminia

Book design by Emanuele Ragnisco
www.mekkanografici.com

Printed in Italy
Arti Grafiche La Moderna – Rome

Chronicles of Dust and Sin
by Paul Bailey*

Alfred Hayes had fallen out of fashion long before he died in 1985 at seventy-four. Yet in the nineteenfifties and sixties he was regarded as one of the most interesting and original American novelists. His British admirers included such variously discerning authors and critics as Angus Wilson, Walter Allen, J. Maclaren-Ross, Antonia White, Francis Wyndham, and Elizabeth Bowen, who described his novella *In Love* as a "little masterpiece." Why, then, has his work disappeared, almost without a trace? The answer has something to do with changing tastes in fiction and even more to do with the increasing reluctance of publishers to keep in print those books on their lists that can never sell in large quantities. Otherwise there is no valid reason to account for his eclipse. At least four of his novels deserve to be reissued. They are so short that they could easily be contained within a single volume that would still weigh far less than John Irving's latest.

Hayes was born in London in 1911, but was raised and educated in New York. After leaving college, he was taken on as a reporter for both the *Daily News* and *The New York American*. He began his serious writing career as a poet and had his poems accepted by *The New Yorker* and several other prestigious magazines. During the Second World War, he served

*Paul Bailey on Alfred Hayes, whose quartet of novels goes to the core of doomed relationships, Saturday, October 29, 2005, *The Guardian*. Paul Bailey's most recent book is *A Dog's Life,* published by Hamish Hamilton (2003).

with the U.S. Special Services in Europe and was stationed in Rome in 1943. It was there that he befriended the film directors Roberto Rossellini, Luigi Zampa, and Vittorio de Sica. He fell in love with the Italian language, which he soon learned to speak fluently. He was given an Oscar nomination, along with the young Federico Fellini, for his work on the script of Rossellini's important second movie, *Paisan,* and he also contributed dialogue to De Sica's *The Bicycle Thief,* for which he was uncredited.

He returned to America in 1945. For the next three decades he was in fairly constant demand as a screenwriter in Hollywood. His credits include Fred Zinneman's *Teresa* (1951), for which he received his second Academy Award nomination, and two films by the great Fritz Lang—*Clash by Night* (1952) and *Human Desire* (1955), a remake of Jean Renoir's classic *La Bête Humaine.* A poem he wrote about the folk singer and socialist militant Joe Hill, who was executed in Utah in 1915, provided the lyrics for the song made famous by Joan Baez and later inspired Bo Widerberg's over-lyrical biopic.

Alfred Hayes's third novel, and the first of the quartet that should be retrieved from obscurity, is *The Girl on the Via Flaminia* (1949). As its title suggests, it is set in Rome, and the girl in question is Lisa, whose friend Nina, a successful whore, persuades her to share a room with a frustrated American soldier named Robert. The room is in an apartment on Via Flaminia owned by the Pulcini family. Signora Adele Pulcini is the most respectable kind of pimp, providing wine and cheese and pasta to the English and American officers who spend their leisure hours and their money in her kitchen. The time is 1944, and the newly liberated city is filled with men desperate for sex. The Roman women are just as desperate for money and food, and prostitution has become almost a regular way of life. Yet this novel is concerned with chastity and the beginnings of love. Lisa and Robert have to pretend to be married.

They sleep in the same double bed, and sleeping is all they are able to do. Lisa makes it clear from the outset that she despises herself for being where she is, in the company of a man who assumes he can pay for his gratification with an abundance of *lire*. The scenes between the disdainful Lisa and the genuinely sensitive Robert are like a series of courtly dances—one step forwards, two steps backwards. They both lose their tempers, and they both try to explain the difficult position they're in.

Lisa's fear of involvement is poignantly delineated, as is Robert's progress from simple lust to worried affection. They are on the verge of forming a deeper relationship when the police arrive to interrogate Signora Pulcini. She tells them that Lisa and Robert are a married couple and have papers to prove it. The policeman leading the investigation asks to examine the papers, and Robert has to lie that they are lodged at his army headquarters. It is then that Lisa goes to the authorities and in a fit of self-loathing has herself registered as an official prostitute. She is tested for venereal disease and is given a clean bill of health. She is handed a special identification card which she must, by law, show to her clients. Now, she reasons, she is properly and finally humiliated. Robert listens to her terrible story, kisses and embraces her and assures her that she will never have to make use of the card.

At last he convinces her of his abiding love, it seems, and at last she responds to his attentiveness. But the novel doesn't end there, with the romantic battle won. Hayes is a master of the narrative that halts or leaps forward to the future rather than concludes. The last two pages of *The Girl on the Via Flaminia* are acutely painful in their uncertainty.

In Love is even shorter than its predecessor, with a smaller cast and a narrower focus. It takes as its epigraph the opening lines of George Herbert's "Love": "Love bade me welcome; yet my soul drew back, / Guilty of dust and sin." The story is told by a man in a hotel bar in New York to an attractive younger woman he has recently met. His chat-up line is unusual, in that it rarely shows him in a favourable light. The man is in his early forties and is still smarting from the pain he was made to endure in the last months of an unhappy love affair.

It is clear from the man's tone that he is cultivated, has read books, looked at pictures and appreciated all kinds of music. The woman he has loved and lost is prone to boredom when she isn't being flattered and wined and dined. She discarded him in the most cavalier and unpleasant manner imaginable, only to invite him back into her life when a new lover refused to marry her.

The grateful narrator drives her to Atlantic City for a romantic weekend, forgetting that the season is over and there are no chalets or cottages to hire. The weather is freezing, there is no heating in the car and she is cold, miserable, and monosyllabic. They pass a ghastly night in an otherwise unoccupied hotel and he makes forceful love to her for the first and last time.

The third doomed liaison is accounted for in *My Face for the World to See* (1958). The man this time is a Hollywood screenwriter who spends four months of each year in California, leaving his wife, Charlotte, in New York. He has rented an apartment from a woman who has "gone off to Europe to forget an unsuccessful marriage which had been followed by an apparently unsuccessful divorce." The book opens with the narrator being bored at a party in Ocean House. To escape all the chatter, he goes out on to the terrace and sees a girl, drink in hand, a "store-bought captain's hat" on her head, walking into the Pacific. He is admiring her body and then he realises that she is about to commit suicide. He rushes down to the beach, hurls himself into the sea and rescues her. It is an act of bravery and decency that he will come to regret as the story unfolds. She is pretty, and it's her prettiness that has brought her to the West Coast. Her single ambition is to become a famous movie star.

She phones her rescuer and thanks him. He is wary and cautious to begin with, sensing that she might be seriously disturbed. She has had screen tests, been invited to recline on the casting couch, and has been involved with a married man.

The reader wants to alert him to the mess that's awaiting him—a mess he is aware of but can't extricate himself from. He tells her something he has told no one else—that he no longer desires the wife he respects. Hayes writes luminously about people who can't help themselves, who can't resist the temptations that are set to destroy them. Walter Allen reviewed the novel in the *New Statesman*, noting: "This author's is a truly formidable and terrifying talent. He has a merciless insight into human behaviour and he writes with extreme compression and great directness." "Merciless" is entirely appropriate, especially in regard to the closing pages when the drunken girl embarrasses him in a restaurant and then slits her wrists behind a locked bathroom door. Here is the glitzy culture that Hayes knew at firsthand and was able to analyse and dissect with lapidary skill. The prose is polished till it shines.

The End of Me, which appeared a decade later, is by far the most bitter and painful of these bitter, painful books. The man, who is in his fifties, is Asher, another Hollywood screenwriter who discovers that his second, greedily ambitious and snobbish wife is conducting an affair with her tennis partner. He flees from their luxurious home, leaving the lights in every room blazing, and returns to his native New York. He visits an elderly aunt who asks him to help her grandson Michael, who ekes out a meagre living but wants to be a published poet. Asher meets Michael and is unaccountably rude to him. He invites the unprepossessing young man back to his hotel and agrees to read his poems. The year is 1968, and the poems are single-mindedly devoted to the sexual act, with "fuck" and "cunt" in constant employment. Asher understands that the poetry is inspired by Michael's girlfriend Aurora, who is of Italian descent. Aurora teases and torments Asher, and, aided and abetted by Michael, orchestrates a series of bizarre events to humiliate him. They know a victim when they see one. The plot is always surprising in this despairing page-turner. What isn't surprising is that *The End of Me* marks Hayes's farewell to the subject of romantic obsession. Asher, looking down at the street, notices his fellow New Yorkers walking by. It is he who has nowhere to go.

I first read Hayes in my twenties, suffering the sorrows and indignities of unrequited love. His books struck a plangent chord. Reading him again, in my sixties, I register that certain aspects of the novels belong to their period—the cocktails, the cigarette lighters, the fact that the men wear hats and that "gay" means "merry." But nothing else is dated. Hayes has done for bruised men what Jean Rhys does for bruised women, and they both write heartbreakingly beautiful sentences.

THE GIRL
ON THE
VIA FLAMINIA

1.

The wind blew through Europe. It was a cold wind, and there were no lights in the city. It was said the cabinet was about to fall. Nobody knew for sure whether the cabinet which was in power at this time would fall and another coalition government would be formed. There was nothing that was very sure, and all one knew was that, if the cabinet did fall, the government which would be formed from the ruins would be another coalition one, and that the wind was cold. It did not look at this time as though the war would end, although actually the war was coming to an end. Nobody knew at this time that the war would end in a few months. There were children in the city who had never known a time in which there had not been a war. The fighting was going on in the north. Sometimes in the afternoon in the city one could see girls and young men standing in the main piazzas wearing red armbands and rough uniforms. Those were the partisans. The men were usually handsomer than the girls were pretty. Everybody looked at them very respectfully. They were part of the real and important fighting that was going on. In the city itself there were many soldiers. The soldiers were of different kinds. The kinds of fighting they did among themselves and the way they got drunk distinguished the soldiers. The English were very fond of fighting with the big steel buckles of their military belts, and the Americans with bottles, and some of the other troops preferred knives. The drunkenness was everywhere. The most conspicuous of the military drunks were the Americans. The Canadians had discovered that vermouth and banana oil made a kind of cocktail but hardly any of the other troops thought so. The Canadians hated the English and envied the Americans. The English envied the Americans and despised the Canadians. The French wore American uniforms and drove in American vehicles and despised the English and shrugged their shoulders at the Canadians and shook their heads in disbelief at the Americans. The lonesomest troops were the Poles and the Palestinian brigadiers.

The cold was really bad. It was December, and almost Christmas, and the war had been going on for over five years. Sometimes men would escape from the prison camps near the Austrian border. They would come home to their wives so terribly changed the women would shriek. There were some husbands, too, who came home to find their wives with other men or with soldiers. That kind of shrieking in the neighborhoods was also bad.

On this December night, the Via Flaminia was very dark, with the wind blowing down its length, and the night was cold with the kind of coldness that in another country would have meant snow. But here in this country there was no snow except on the mountains. There was rain, and fog, and the damp cold.

In this section of the city the people before the war had not been too rich or too poor. Now, of course, after more than five years of war, they were all more or less poor. The poverty was not of money. In this section of the city there were apartment houses with enormous windows and visible roof gardens. The trolley line went down to the end of the street which was the Via Flaminia and then crossed the Ponte Milvio which was a very old and very much-used bridge and from there the road went up north. During the day there were always accidents on the streets. Pedestrians were killed or hurt with a deadly regularity coming across the bridge or across the Via Flaminia, and they were usually killed or hurt by large fast six- or eight-wheeled military vehicles. The citizens, when there was such an accident, always cursed the fate which had brought the military vehicles to the city, and the dead or dying man would lie in the gutter covered with a blanket or an overcoat until an ambulance and a carabiniere would arrive to take him away to a hospital. Since there were no medicines in the hospitals, the man would often be considered lucky if he died en route. The blood would remain in a thick pool in the gutter.

In one of the apartment houses in that section of the city where the Via Flaminia crossed the Milvio bridge there was a flat in which a family known as the Pulcinis lived. It was a flat of six rooms, and the dining room which was large had been converted by the Signora Adele Pulcini into a place where the soldiers came at night for wine and eggs. There was a big mahogany table in the center of the dining room, a radio which the soldiers liked to have playing music as they drank, and on the wall, of course, there was a lithograph of a Sacred Heart. A French door led out of the dining room into a small shabby garden and to a back gate. The soldiers called the Signora Adele Pulcini "Mamma." And one night, toward the end of December, as the war unknowingly was coming to its hoped-for end, two soldiers were sitting at the big mahogany table in the Pulcini's apartment, drinking wine. One of the soldiers was a short, wiry, middle-aged English sergeant, and the other was an American, a young American, who was not a sergeant, but who was very flushed with wine, and who walked with a very slight limp.

It was about seven-thirty in the evening.

The middle-aged English sergeant had been listening for some time to the complaints of the young American who was not a sergeant. The Englishman did not think that anyone in the American army had a thing to complain about. The Englishman loved his country but not his country's rations. The

Englishman often said, when he was thoroughly disgusted with the slice of bread and the slice of spam served in the sergeants' mess where, as an English sergeant, he had the luxury of being able to sit down at a long rough board table with seven other sergeants, that more than once he thought of going absent up into the hills to live with the bloody partigianos. Now, in the dining room, with a glass of wine in his hand, he said to the young American, "What're you blokes got to grouse about? Gawd," the Englishman said, "you ought t' be in His Majesty's fightin' forces for a bloody month, and chew our bully, and wash it down with a cup o' stinking tea, and be happy when they puts a bit o' marmalade on the bread, and then you'd have something to write home about."

"Beef to the brass," the American said.

"Ay," the Englishman said. "Scum o' the earth, her ladyship called us. Stood up she did, in the House o' Commons, and said it: scum o' the earth. An' bloody right she was."

The American limped slightly as he went toward the door. The door opened into a hallway, and the other rooms in the flat were off the hallway.

"Hey, Mamma!" the American called. "Mamma Pulcini! How about a bottle of vino? Subito!"

"Sì, sì," a woman's voice replied from the kitchen. "Un momento."

"Everything in this country's un momento," the American said. He limped back toward the table. He wore a wristwatch and a ring made of an Arabian coin and an identification bracelet. It looked like a great deal of jewelry. "How did I wind up in Italy?" he said to the English sergeant. "I wanted to go to France. My old man was in France in the last one. You ever go with a French broad, sarge?"

"No," the Englishman said.

"I met a sailor was in Marseilles," the American said. "He had a girl named Marie. He says when he was in Marseilles he

used to sleep in her house, and in the morning her mother used
to serve him breakfast in bed. They weren't even married, and
she was only eighteen years old. How do you like that?"

"Eighteen," the English sergeant said. "Me missus is twice
eighteen."

"France, that would have been for me," the American said.

"Oh," the sergeant said, "Rome ain't bad."

"Rome's a city," the American said. "Cities are different. But
you take the rest of the country. Mountains!"

"Well, it's a pretty country, except for the flies."

"Listen, sarge," the American said. "Know what they can do
with Europe? All of it? Fold it three ways and ram it. Listen. I
walked up here from Anzio. Then at Velletri I fell off a cliff. In
the dark! Fell off a cliff and bust my ankle."

He pulled up the leg of his trousers.

"Feel that," he said to the Englishman. "Feel that ankle."

Solicitously, the Englishman touched the stockinged bone.

"Here?" he asked.

"Right there," the soldier said. "Feel it?"

"Bit o' somethin' stickin' out," the Englishman said.

"That's where it's bust," the soldier said. "Off a goddam cliff
in Velletri in the dark. But nobody believes me. Everybody
thinks I'm trying to goof off from my outfit. Could I go back
to my outfit with an ankle bust like that?"

He looked at the sergeant unhappily. The sergeant poured a
glass of wine.

"I saw a chap once had his whole foot smashed," the sergeant said. "Bloody gun fell on him."

The Signora Adele Pulcini came into the dining room. She
was a tall woman, with gray hair, in her fifties, and her face was
sharp and dark. She was dressed in black, and a cigarette was
in the corner of her mouth. At night she lay in bed, with the
electric light on, smoking cigarettes and coughing. She looked
at the two soldiers in the room, and she said to the American,

"Imbecille! How many times have I told you not to shout? Twice last week the carabinieri came in . . ."

"Come here, Mamma," the American said to the Signora Pulcini. "Feel this ankle."

"Ankle?" the tall hard-faced woman said. "What ankle?"

"Feel it," the American said.

The Signora Pulcini accommodatingly felt his ankle.

"So?" she said.

"Busted," the soldier said. "Off a cliff in Velletri. That's what I got liberating your goddam city."

"Peccato," the woman said.

"Could I march with an ankle like that, busted?" the soldier said. "Could I, Mamma?"

"Of course not," the Signora Pulcini said, knowing that one must always agree with the soldiers who came to drink in her dining room on those nights when the city was dark and cold and lonely. "You are a very brave soldier."

"I'd have gone back to my outfit," the American said. "It wasn't I didn't want to. I came up with them from Oran. I went through Venafro with them. We hit the beach together. But the medics reassigned me. They could see I couldn't do the walking anymore."

"Of course," Adele Pulcini said, seeing how agitated he was, and how inside him something hurt, and knowing that the soldiers could be ugly and dangerous when the things inside them began to hurt. "Now sit down," she said. "Mimi will bring the wine."

She, too, went to the door and called, but not loudly, "Mimi!"

From the kitchen a girl's voice, very light and quick, answered, "Sì, signora?"

"Fai presto," the tall woman in black said.

"Sì, signora," the girl's voice replied. "Vengo subito."

Adele Pulcini turned to her two soldiers. "In this house," she said, smiling, "we are all heroes."

"Bloody heroes," the English sergeant said.

Mimi entered the dining room, carrying a bottle of wine. It was a red wine made in the hills. The wine sparkled in the light. Mimi was sixteen. She enjoyed the soldiers, and she respected and was somewhat afraid of the Signora Pulcini. It was not that the signora was not kind. She was kind, but the kindness had a harsh quality, and Mimi would be frightened hearing the signora cough at night in the bedroom. The cough was frightening because the electricity would be on in the bedroom, and the signora would be lying in bed, fully clothed, in her black dress, smoking and coughing. It was impossible to know what the signora thought when she lay like that in bed with all the bedroom lights on.

When the American who limped saw Mimi he put his two hands over his heart like an opera singer, and said, "Bella mia."

Little Mimi giggled.

She said to the Signora Pulcini, in her own language, "Is he crazy?"

"Sì," Adele said. "A little. Put down the bottle."

"Sì, signora," Mimi said, setting the bottle of wine on the dining room table.

"What did she say?" the American asked.

"She asked if you are crazy," Adele answered.

"We're all crazy, honey," the American who limped said. "The crazy Americans."

Mimi giggled at the soldier.

"That is true," she said to Adele.

"Yes," Adele said, "that is absolutely true."

"Come on, bella mia," the American said to the little girl. "We dance. American tip-top ballerino."

"Have I permission?" Mimi asked.

"Sì," the Signora Pulcini said. "Dance with him. He is drunk."

"Who's ubriaco?" the American said. "I ain't ubriaco."

"Hokay," Mimi said in English. "I danze."

They danced. The radio played, the wind blew against the wooden shutters, the Englishman poured himself another glass of wine, and the tall woman in the corner of whose eyes there were so many dark wrinkles smiled a little thinly as she watched her maid dance with the drunken and clumsy soldier.

The Englishman tasted the wine.

"Scum o' the earth she called us," he said, "her ladyship. Right in the House o' Commons."

He should have gone absent up into the bloody hills with the partigianos. It was almost Christmas and it was a good thing his missus wasn't in London. From London, now the air raids were over, there were reports of the big buzz bombs, and that was worse, his missus wrote, than the raids.

Another girl came into the dining room. She was very red-haired, and very trim, and she wore high-heeled shoes. In the wintertime hardly any of the women of the city, even when they could afford it, wore high-heeled shoes. In America, of course, the women wore them, and in Paris. Nina wore them, too. They had been bought for her in a smart shop by an American captain. She had been very grateful to the captain the night the shoes were purchased. Now, with the shoes, she wore a bright tight silk print dress, with a red leather belt around her small waist, and she was carrying a valise. She put the valise down on the floor. The silk dress fell away from her breasts.

"Adele," Nina said, "did she come?"

"Not yet," the Signora Pulcini said.

"I'm all packed," Nina said. She looked at her wristwatch. "Why doesn't she come?"

The American who limped deserted little Mimi. "Bella mia!" he said to the red-haired girl with the valise.

She slapped his reaching hand.

"Proibito," she said.

"What's the valise for?" the soldier asked.

"Nina goes to Florence," the Signora Pulcini said.

"To Florence?" the American said. "What's in Florence?"

"Love, caro mio," Nina said. "Love, love, love."

"Hell," the American said, "in Rome there's love, love, love too."

"She is engaged to an American," Adele said. "A capitano. He takes her to Florence."

"An officer?"

"The most beautiful officer," Nina said.

"Beautiful," the American said. "How the hell can he be beautiful and an officer?"

"He is not like you, lazzarone," Nina said. She was very gay. She patted the silk down on her hips. "He is gentle . . . so polite! When he smiles, madonna, such teeth! Let me see your teeth."

The soldier bared his teeth for her.

"With teeth like that you stay in Rome."

"Let me take you to Florence," the soldier said.

"We'll go live in a palazzo. I know a guy in Florence lives in a palazzo. We'll borrow the palazzo from him."

"No," Nina said. "My captain respects Italian girls."

"Me, too," the soldier said. "I respect Italian girls."

"Sì. A letto."

"What's a letto?"

"In bed."

"Well," the American said, "that's a great place to respect them, ain't it?"

"No, no!" Nina said. "You are pretty, but not like my babbee . . ."

"I'm as good as your babbee . . ."

"Impossible!"

"Try me," the soldier said. "I'm terrific. Ain't I terrific, England?"

"Smashin'," the Englishman said.

"See that?" the soldier said. "I'm smashin'."

"No, no!" Nina said, gayly.

"I busted an ankle in Velletri liberating Roma bella," the soldier said, "and I'm seven thousand miles from Schenectady, and it's a cold night. Where's your gratitude?"

"Ah, babbee, I am so sorry for you," Nina said, patting his cheek. "But you do not have teeth like my captain."

She turned to the Signora Pulcini.

"Call me when Lisa comes," she said.

She waved to the soldier. "Ciao," she said, "poor babbee," and she went out of the room.

When she was gone, the American looked unhappily at the sergeant. "Aw, they save it for the brass," he said. He looked at Adele Pulcini. "Don't you know a girl, Mamma, who wants to have dinner with a sad soldato?"

"Always the girls," the tall woman said.

"What else is there?" the soldier said. "I just want a place I can take her."

"You have a girl home," Mamma Pulcini said.

"That's Schenectady," the soldier said.

"But you make trouble," the woman said. "You Americans always make trouble."

"I won't make no trouble, Mamma, honest to god," the soldier said. "Why should I make trouble?"

The signora looked at him doubtfully. "You will be nice to the girl?"

"Sure!"

"It may not be possible . . ."

"Try," the soldier said. "I got money. Look at the money I got." He took a thick bunch of lire from his pocket. "What am I going to do with my goddam dough? Save it until I get back to Schenectady? Go on, Mamma. Call me a girl."

"Va bene," the tall woman said. "But it's only because I have pity for you."

"Sure," the soldier said.

"And remember—no trouble!"

"Honest to god!" the soldier said.

He was excited now. He followed the tall dark woman in the black dress to the telephone which stood on the bureau. He said to her, eagerly, "What is she; Mamma? A blonde? Does she talk English? What's her name?"

"Maria," the signora said.

She dialed the phone.

"Pronto," she said into the telephone. "Chi parla? Maria? Ciao, Maria." She spoke for a while into the phone. "This," she said to Maria, "is the Signora Pulcini. Sì. Come va?" There was, in her house, now, an American, who was lonely, and who wanted to make an appointment. Yes, for this evening, she said. Yes, un soldato americano. Yes, a little drunk, but not bad, not too bad, he had promised to make no trouble. She glanced at the soldier. His face had a muddy and excited look. She noticed the thickening effect the drinking of so much wine had given his face. She noticed how the hair was cut short like an athlete's.

She said to the listening soldier. "Where will you take her, she asks?"

"Any place she wants to go," the soldier said eagerly. "Tell her a restaurant. Ask her if she likes spaghetti."

"She prefers meat," Adele said.

"All right, meat," the soldier said. "She can have anything she wants."

"Va bene," the tall woman said into the phone. "Ciao, Maria." She hung up.

"Is it all fixed?" the soldier asked. "Did you fix it for me, Mamma?"

They are so young, Adele thought, and they are so eager for the girls.

"Sì," she said. "I will give you the address. On the Viale Angelico. You know where?"

"I'll find it," the soldier said.

"You go across the bridge and follow the Lungotevere," Adele said.

"I'll find it all right, I'll find it," the soldier said.

She wrote out the address for him on the back of an old envelope. The wind blew against the window panes and shook the wooden shutters.

The English sergeant emptied his glass of wine. There was a sour and puckered taste in his mouth. Back in his barracks he had nailed a picture of his wife to the wall above his bed. He would look at the picture and say, "Well, neither of us are a ravin' beauty," and then he would think of the incredible length of time he had not seen London. The beds in the barracks were two-bunk affairs, of wood, and there were no mattresses. There were seven other sergeants in the small room with him. The other ranks slept in a big common loft on beds which were made of wooden slats and wire. Because he was a sergeant, he had a double bunk and he slept in a room that housed only seven other sergeants. The officer he drove for slept in a big hotel on the Via Veneto. The English sergeant stood up.

"Time I went too," he said.

"Grazie, Mamma," the American said. He held the envelope with Maria's address. He was very pleased with the address. He was anxious now to find the house on the Viale Angelico.

"Go out through the back," the Signora Pulcini said, somewhat glad they were going. "I do not want you seen leaving the house. Come, I'll open the gate."

They went together to the French door in the rear of the dining room. The Englishman humped his shoulders into the warmth of his overcoat. "In the House o' Commons," he muttered, "she stood up, her ladyship . . ."

They went out into the darkness and the cold.

The room was quiet.

2.

The doorbell rang.

There was the sound of the door being opened, and of Mimi's voice asking a question, then Mimi came into the dining room, and a girl was with her. "Sit down, signora," Mimi said. "I will call Nina."

"Grazie," the girl said.

When Mimi had gone, the girl looked about the room. She was a pretty girl, rather tall, with good shoulders, and soft blonde hair. She wore a raincoat, a gray wool skirt, a wool sweater and, because of the cold, thick white ski stockings and walking shoes with tasseled laces. She sat in the room, looking at the mahogany table on which the wine still stood where the English sergeant had left it, the radio, the lithograph of the pierced and bleeding heart. The look she gave the objects in the room was that of someone who did not like what she saw and yet was curious about the very objects that she disapproved of. From the garden, bringing a blast of coldness with her, Adele Pulcini opened the French door and entered the room. She saw the girl in the raincoat sitting there.

"Buona sera," Adele said. "Che brutto tempo fuori. What ugly weather. Even the winters are worse." She looked inquiringly at the girl.

"I am Lisa Costa," the girl said.

The Signora Pulcini smiled. "But of course," she said. "We were expecting you. Does Nina know you are here?"

"The little girl went to call her," Lisa said.

Adele went to the door.

"Nina!" she called into the hallway. "The Signora Lisa is here."

From her room, Nina answered: "I am coming . . . in a minute . . ."

Adele turned. "And your husband," she said, "he is with you?"

The girl looked up quickly.

"My . . . ?"

"The American," Adele said. "Your husband. He is with you?"

"No," the girl said. "He is not with me right now."

"Eh, you girls," Adele said, lighting a cigarette. "All of you marrying Americans. Suddenly, all the women in Rome love Americans. But . . . it's smart . . ."

"Smart?" the girl said.

"Yes," Adele said, smiling, for it was a kind of understanding between all the women of Europe now, the thing about Americans. "Escape, my dear. Escape! What's left of Europe? A memory. If I were twenty, I'd do exactly what you've done."

"Would you?" the girl said softly, looking across the table at her.

"Of course!" Adele said. "If I were twenty, of course. He will take you to America when the war's over. Go! Escape, my dear. Out of this misery. Out of this darkness. Europe is finished. It will never be again what it was."

She tapped the cigarette lightly into the tray on the dining-room table.

"How ugly life is now," she said, thinking of the wind blowing, the blackness of the streets between the cold houses. She herself would survive, of course; she had always survived; she was all leather and insomnia. But the others, they were weaker, they could not tolerate the difficulties, they were not hard enough, there was not enough leather and iron in them. "This

house," she said. "At night the soldiers come—they are lonesome, they come to sit at Mamma Pulcini's. They drink, I cook
an egg if they're hungry, they listen to the music from the radio.
It pleases them to be inside a house, and the egg I cook tastes
better than the eggs of the army, and they enjoy eating it on a
dining-room table even though they have to pay for it, and the
egg may not be as fresh. One has only to be a little careful of
the carabinieri . . ."

"And your husband?" the girl asked.

"My husband? Now and then he works—at the National
Bank of Labor . . . I have a son, too—" she shook her head.
"So—one lives . . ."

Nina came into the dining room.

"Darling!" she said.

She went to the table and kissed the blonde girl. "You've
met Adele . . . ?"

"Yes," Lisa said.

"You'll like the room," Nina said. "Won't she like the room,
Adele?"

"I had Mimi clean it thoroughly," Adele said. "The Americans like everything clean."

"You'll like it, you'll be very comfortable," Nina said. "You
were lucky I met you and I'm going to Florence. Try finding an
apartment in the city now."

"Apartments are difficult because of the bombings," Adele
said. "Everybody thinks Rome is safe."

"Yes," the girl said. "The Pope protects us, doesn't he?"

"Well," Adele said, "one must be grateful to the priests for
something."

"It's all settled about the room," Nina said. "You'll be very
happy, darling, and I'll say addio Roma!" She looked at her
friend. " Let me see you." She held up Lisa's chin. "Isn't she
beautiful, Adele?"

"She has a very pretty skin," Adele said.

"She has wonderful shoulders," Nina said. "You should see her naked. Her shoulders are wonderful. But her hair is what I envy most. Wait until my captain discovers mine isn't really this color."

"A tragedy," Adele said.

"He'll die," Nina said, "when it comes out black again . . ."

"Then leave it red."

"At five hundred lire a rinse?"

"He's an American," Adele said. "He can afford it."

"Won't it be difficult," Lisa asked, "your going to Florence now?"

"Why?"

"It's forbidden for civilians to travel without a permit," Lisa said. "But I suppose for a soldier . . ."

"Not a soldier, cara," Nina said. "An officer. In the American army there's a great difference."

"Eh. . ." Adele said. "Love, love!"

"Don't be silly, Adele," Nina said. "They serve magnificent breakfasts, the Americans."

"While we have nothing," Lisa said.

"One can always eat," Nina said.

"They say," Adele said, "the Americans eat four times a day."

"They live well."

"What a country it must be, their America," Adele said.

"An Italian discovered it," Lisa said.

"And the English stole it," Adele said.

"What hasn't the Italian lost?" Nina said.

"I was telling the Signora Lisa how lucky she is," Adele said, looking at the girl with her hard black eyes. "After the war she will be able to go to America."

"Of course," Nina said, quickly. "That's the advantage of having wonderful shoulders."

"Where were you married, my dear?" Adele asked. "In Rome?"

"In Napoli," Nina said.

"Really?"

"Yes," Lisa said, pausing. "In Napoli."

"Bella Napoli," Adele said. "Is it as destroyed as they say?"

"Terribly."

"Once upon a time," Adele said, "how they sang!"

"Well," Nina said, "they don't sing now."

"Yes," Adele said, thinking of the lost songs.

"Povera Italia . . ."

"Poveri noi," Lisa said.

"Adele," Nina said. "Go make a cup of coffee. I must have a cup of coffee before I go."

"Real coffee?" Lisa said.

"From Nina's captain," Adele replied.

"Oh."

"What will we do when she goes?" Adele said, standing up. "My husband without his coffee!"

"Lisa's Roberto will bring you American coffee," Nina said.

"Is his name Roberto?"

"Sì."

The girl looked up questioningly at Nina. "Without his coffee my husband's lost," Adele said. She went out of the room. Outside, in the darkness, the trolleys were stalled in their barns, and on the Corso, in the shadow of the galleria, where the newspaper stand was, boarded up, there were sinister figures, indistinct and muffled. The police patrolled the boulevards in small squads of three, with slung carbines, and there were lights in the lower rooms of the questura where the detectives played cards. In the dining room here, in the flat on the Via Flaminia, Nina now turned to the girl who sat, her hands in the pockets of her raincoat. "I'm exhausted," Nina said. "Such a day. Such excitement."

The blonde girl's voice was very low.

"When will he come?" she asked.

"Who?"

"Your Roberto," she said.

"Mine?" Nina said. "Yours, dear."

"When will he come?" Lisa said.

On the hills above the city the trees were thinned out of the forests because the Germans had cut so much firewood during the occupation, and in the nursery, which had once been the villa of the dictator, the orphaned children slept, in their uniform nightgowns, in a long room with many mirrors. The mirrors had once witnessed other sleepers.

Nina looked at her. "I telephoned," she said. "Dio! To telephone an American! First one answers: who do I want? I say il sergente Roberto. Roberto? What Roberto? They never heard of a Roberto in their company. Oh, he says, the one who answers—Bob! Sì, Bob! Well, he says, this one on the telephone, how about me, babbee, instead of Bob? Finally he goes. Va bene. Another one comes to the telephone. Again who do I want. Again the Roberto, again the Bob. Then he says: 'allo, 'allo, who is speaking? Nina. Nina! this one shouts, on the telephone. How's the old tomato? Che pomodoro? Who has a tomato? But that is how one telephones an American."

"And when you spoke to him?" the girl asked.

"Who?"

"Roberto."

Nina shrugged. "He was happy you had agreed. Why shouldn't he be? Look how pretty his girl will be . . ."

"Pretty," the girl said.

"But you are pretty," Nina said, admiring her.

"Yes, and this is pretty too," Lisa said. "To wait, like this, in a strange house for a man I've never seen."

"Why do you have to see him? If he's nice, he's nice, sight unseen." She looked at the girl again. There was a sound of the wind in the garden. Wine lay in the bottom of the glass on the table. "Listen to me, cara," Nina said. She put her ringed hands on the girl's shoulders. She could feel the strong bones under the raincoat and under the sweater. "Roberto's a good boy. He's intelligent, he's not bad looking, he's not an animal like some of the others. For three weeks he's bothered me to introduce him to a nice girl. Have you eaten today?"

"It's not important," Lisa said.

"Have you paid your rent?"

The girl was silent.

"So. At least with Roberto you'll eat, and you'll have somewhere to live. I've told Adele you are married to him. I've explained to Roberto how it will be—that you're not a street girl, and that the arrangement will be a permanent one. He's anxious, too. The army's a cold place, and you're pretty."

"But I can't," the girl said, twisting away.

"You can't what?"

"I can't make love to a stranger."

Nina looked at her. The light lay softly on the blonde hair, and she thought how soft the hair looked, how soft the skin was. "One learns," she said.

"Oh, Nina . . ."

"What do you want me to say? One learns. One learns everything. Wars are all the same. The men become thieves, and the women—" She shrugged her narrow expressive shoulders. "And it's the same everywhere."

"Not in America," the girl said.

"In America, too, if they had gone through what we've gone through. No," she said, "one doesn't live as one likes to, but as one must. Go through the city. On the Corso, on the Via Veneto, on all the bridges—it's the same. Everywhere the soldiers and the women. Why? Because there is nothing else, cara mia, except to drink and to make love and to survive. And our men? Poof! Their guts are gone. Let them whimper and shout—the cigarettes they smoke, and the coffee they drink, we buy them."

"I'm not one of the women who stand on the bridges," the girl said.

"Did I say you were?" Nina said. "We are all unlucky in the same way. We were born, and born women, and in Europe, during the wars. Ah, Lisa, it's all the same I tell you—for you or the contessa, in her elegant apartment, sleeping with some English colonel or some American brigadier! What do you think the contessa calls it? It's an arrangement—it's love . . . but she, too, needs sugar and coffee when she wakes up in a cold room. Everything now is such an arrangement. Besides, who will it harm? Adele will have her rent—and if you won't be happier, at least you won't be hungrier . . ."

"But what will I say to him?" the girl said.

"Madonna!" Nina said.

"I've never gone with a soldier," the girl said.

"Ask him how's his old tomato," Nina said. "Dio, you've talked to a man before."

"Not one of the Americans."

"They speak exactly the same language."

"Yes," Lisa said. "The liberators."

Nina gestured. "We lost the war, my dear."

"Only the war?" the girl said.

"Oh, you make me sick!"

"Yes," the girl said, staring at the wine glass on the table, "he'll feed me because he's won the war, and that's part of the arrangement, and then after he's fed me we'll go to bed, because that's part of the arrangement, too." She turned her head slowly, as though she were trapped in the room. "But why should I be better or different than the others standing on the bridges waiting for their soldiers? I'll have my American. Everybody has one now."

"No," Nina said, "you'll jump in the Tiber."

"Why not?"

"So they'll fish out another fool."

"There will be one less in the world."

"I ought to let you!"

"It's not important either way," the girl said.

"Except," Nina said angrily, leaning toward her, "I went through all the trouble of getting you a nice one."

The girl's face was averted. "You take him," she said. "You like Americans."

"Like them?" Nina laughed. "Some I could spit on. You should see their officers as I've seen them . . . what animals! Screaming in the hotel corridors, and such jokes! To them it's a wonderful joke to hang toilet paper from a chandelier!"

"They're gay," the girl said. "For them it's a gay war."

"No," Nina said, "not really; they're not really gay. Really they're a gloomy people, the Americans . . ."

"And your captain?"

"That's something else."

"Will he marry you?"

"The man has a wife somewhere. Ohio . . . and she's cold and ungrateful and extravagant . . ."

"Why doesn't he divorce her?"

"Oh," Nina said, "it's wonderful how many cold wives the Americans have they do not divorce!"

"Che brutta guerra," the girl said.

"Si. But what shall I do—cry my eyes out? Or jump in the Tiber? There's enough corpses on the bottom now . . . and it's better to eat and to go to Florence when one can . . ."

"Or wait," the girl said, "in a house for some Roberto . . ."

"Yes, even to wait in a house for some Roberto," Nina said.

"But," the girl said.

"But what?"

"He may not like me." Nina looked at her, and smiled slightly. The light lay on the fine skin. Her hair shadowed her eyes.

"My dear," she said, "would you like to bet?"

3

"Eccolo!" Adele said, coming in through the doorway, carrying a tray. "The coffee . . ."

The coffee steamed on the tray.

Behind Adele appeared a tall thin old man, a newspaper tucked under his arm. His spectacles sat on his forehead. He looked into the room.

"You are still here?" Ugo Pulcini said to Nina. "I thought you'd already be high in the mountains."

"My husband," Adele said. "This is the Signora Lisa. She is taking Nina's room."

"Ah," Ugo said, "with the American husband." He came into the room. "In Milan once—before the war, it was all before the war—I knew an American girl. A schoolteacher. At the Hotel Tuscania . . ."

"So!" Adele said, looking at her husband.

He smiled, deprecatingly. "An old transgression, my dear . . . 1920! She was making a summer tour. I remember she ate little sandwiches, and in the hotel there was a bar with a special fountain for American schoolteachers . . . a bar with carbonated water and ice cream . . ."

"Did she enjoy her tour, Ugo?" Nina asked.

"It was 1920 . . . a quarter of a century ago! Besides, I had a great curiosity about American women."

"Did you satisfy it?" Adele said.

"To an extent, my dear: to an extent." He sighed. "You see how far back I have to go to find a pleasant memory?"

"Drink your coffee, Don Giovanni," Adele said.

"Now, of course, the tours are different," Ugo said, sitting down. He sighed again, thinking perhaps of the carbonated water. "There are no more schoolteachers who eat little sandwiches at the Hotel Tuscania . . . now there are only soldiers who scratch their names on the walls of the Colosseum. Yes, among the names of the martyrs, and the ghosts of the great gladiators, their names, and some obscure village they come from."

"My husband talks," Adele said to Lisa, apologetically. "He talked himself into the Regina Coeli once."

"Have you been in prison, Signor Pulcini?" the girl asked.

"My dear, we have all been in prison," Ugo said. "It was not too unpleasant. My wife used to come with chicken soup . . ."

"While he played cards in his cell," Adele said.

"She resents my martyrdom," Ugo said, smiling. "Well, one makes all sorts of mistakes in one lifetime." He looked at Nina. "Would you possess, my dear," he said elegantly, "an American cigarette? All day I've smoked nothing but Nazionali."

"For a martyr?" Nina said.

"Perhaps," Ugo said gently, "I should fall in love with a captain?"

"Or a schoolteacher."

"Eh, my schoolteacher days are over," the old man said. He took a cigarette from Nina's extended pack, and lit it. Smoke flowed from his thin nostrils. "Even a cigarette has become a luxury in Europe," he said.

Outside, in the hallway, the doorbell rang again.

"Ah!" Nina said, hearing the bell. "Finalmente!"

She went out quickly into the hail.

Ugo smiled at the blonde girl. "Your husband, signora, does he like Italy?"

She was looking toward the door.

"I don't know," she said.

He came into the room, smiling at them because he was not sure of his reception, and because they were strangers, carrying a musette bag, a little wary, a little uncomfortable, with Nina holding his arm. "Ecco," she said, "the husband!"

He looked at them and at the girl. He was not quite sure yet, and he was being careful, and he was being polite. "Buona sera," he said.

"Signor Pulcini . . . Signora Pulcini . . ." Nina said, beside him, and he smiled again at the tall dark woman with the gray hair and the black dress, and at the old man holding the cigarette elegantly between his thumb and forefinger. The girl in the raincoat had not moved, and she did not smile. "This is Roberto," Nina said. "Guarda! Isn't he intelligent looking for an American? And such a mouth!" She sniffed at him. "How many cognacs did you have?"

"One," the soldier said.

"One?"

"And a chaser."

"What chaser?"

"A cognac."

"You must make him stop drinking, Lisa," Nina said. "None of them will have stomachs by the time they go home."

"I was asking your wife, Signor Roberto," Ugo said, "just before you came if you liked Italy."

He glanced again at the silent girl. He did not know how much was understood among them, and he was not sure of the kind of house he had come to.

"Do I?" he said to the girl sitting there in that taut quietness at the table.

She still did not smile.

"Do you?" she said.

"Yes," the soldier said. "I think it's pretty nice."

"But very much destroyed, no?" Ugo asked.

"No," the soldier said. "Surprisingly. I didn't expect it to be

as nice as it is." He slipped the musette bag from his shoulder.
"As a matter of fact," he said carefully, "it's much prettier than
I thought it would be. Much more." He hoped she understood, for Italy now was much more beautiful than he had
thought coming across the Ponte Milvio in the cold, looking
for a house on the Via Flaminia. And he thought, by the quick
glance she gave him, that perhaps she had understood, and he
hoped that she was pleased.

Behind him, now, somebody said, "Mamma," and then a
young man come into the room. He was handsome, intense,
and he was very tightly belted into an almost bleached raincoat. He stopped as he saw the strangers. "Scusate . . ."

"This is my son, Antonio," Adele said.

Nina glanced again at her expensive wristwatch.

"Dio, the time! My captain'll kill me." She went quickly to
Lisa and kissed her. "Until I return," she said. She shook hands
with Ugo and Adele. "Arrivederci."

"Remember," Ugo said, "it's cold in the mountains."

"Come," Nina said to Antonio. "I'll kiss you too."

"No, grazie," the boy said.

"Not even a little one?"

"Save it for the Allcati," Antonio said.

She turned. "What a grateful son you have," she said to
Adele.

"I kissed better girls in Libya," the boy said.

"But dirtier," Nina answered.

"Only their skin," Antonio said.

"Are you insulting me, darling?" Nina said.

"Who could insult you, carissima?" the boy said. Nina
shrugged; he was obviously hopeless, and she was late.
"Arrivederci, Roberto," she said, touching Robert's arm.

"Good-by, Nina," the soldier said. He looked at her. "And
thanks."

"Be good to her," Nina said. "She has wonderful shoulders.

Come, help me, Adele." She picked up her valise. "Addio," she said once more, and she went out of the dining room, and they could hear her voice, talking incessantly to Adele until the front door slammed.

"Florence," Ugo said, after a little pause. "How far is it? A hundred and fifty kilometers. But now it's a tremendous journey."

Robert took a pack of cigarettes out of his shirt pocket. He held the pack toward the old man. "Cigarette?"

"Ah, grazie." Ugo broke the cigarette carefully into two parts. "Half for now, half for later," he said. He put the second half into the pocket of his vest.

Robert extended the pack now toward Antonio.

"Smoke?"

The boy, belted so dramatically into his bleached raincoat, his smooth black hair combed to a peak on the nape of his neck, drew a blue and crumpled pack from his own pocket. "I prefer our own," he said deliberately.

"Nazionali?" Robert said. "They're pretty bad, aren't they?"

"But they are ours," the boy said.

Robert glanced up into the tense and dark face. He drew his own pack of cigarettes back. He allowed himself to smile a little. The old man drew luxuriously on the half of the cigarette between his lips.

"What a day it was," he said, "the day you took Rome. What a celebration. Were you here, Signor Roberto, then?"

"Yes," Robert said. "I was here."

"What a festa!" Ugo said, shaking his head. "Do you remember, Antonio, how at three o'clock in the morning the people were dancing in the streets? Nobody could sleep."

"Perhaps we celebrated too soon," Antonio said.

But the old man was remembering; six months had gone by, and now, in the streets, the vivas painted on the outer walls of the Vatican were fading, the names of the martyrs were fading, the proclamations and the posters with the clenched fists and the squadrons of planes in the painted sky were torn and shredded by the cold wind; and the cabinet was falling, and eggs were thirty lire an egg. "I remember," the old man said, "at midnight on the third of June . . . all day the Germans going by, out of the city—and a truck burning . . . and a militiaman painting out the big M on his motorcycle and putting in its place a white star. Soldiers and machines, all going north . . . Then in the morning the guns again, closer . . . and then at night nobody sleeping, nobody could rest . . . And that evening—do you remember, Antonio?—in our doorway fell a wounded German. Ich will wasser, hilf mir, hilf mir! . . . All blood up here in the shoulder, and Antonio would not go out of the house to give him water . . ."

"I'd spit in his mouth," the boy said. "That's the water I'd give a German."

"But I took a rag, and wet it, and squeezed the water between his lips," Ugo said. "Why?" He shrugged. "I did not like him dying in the doorway. Then in the evening, dark, I'm in the house, and it's one o'clock . . . I slept, dreaming, and then there's a noise outside the window. I stuck my head out. Outside, on the street, an armored car. I thought—a German? Or perhaps . . . perhaps! And I ran out into the street. What is it? I shouted: English? And somebody shouted: No, no, Americano! And the men are from Chicago! A thousand things ran through my head . . . to call Adele . . . to lock the door . . . and I shouted, because I could think of nothing else to shout: Viva la Chicago!"

The stub of the cigarette had burned down between his fingers, and now, forgetting he was to save the other, he took the broken half from his vest pocket. "What a celebration! What a festa it was that day!" He put the small stub gently and carefully between his lips, nodding at the great memory, the unforgettable experience.

But the boy stood there, in the belted almost white raincoat. "Yes," he said. "We are liberated." He drew on the Nazionale. "We are liberated, aren't we, Signor?" he said to Robert.

"Sure," Robert said.

He made a sudden, almost convulsive movement, pulling the cigarette from his mouth. He crushed it into an ashtray. "You're quite right," he said. "Our cigarettes, they stink." He looked at his father. "What a festa we're having now," he said. "Excuse me . . ." and Robert watched him, with high hunched shoulders and the bitter angry young face under the meticulous haircomb, go abruptly out of the room; and then the old man, troubled, followed the boy out. What was incredible, Robert thought, in the small silence, was that it was only six months ago that Ugo had shouted "Viva la Chicago"; six months, it was only six months. The difference, he thought, was that now you came on a cold extinguished night to a house like this, and there was a girl there, waiting, and an arrangement of a kind. Yes: the difference was that now it was all deals and arrangements, and he had made one, too, for his own reasons. "Six months," he said aloud. "You wouldn't think it was that short a time."

"What?" he heard the girl at the table ask.

"The liberation," he said. "It's only six months. We're coming to the first Christmas we've had since it."

"Have you been in Italy long?" she said.

"Long enough," he answered. And then realized they had been talking; and that he still knew nothing about her, nothing at all, and he did not actually know whether she had accepted, and how he was to proceed if she had, and why she did not do something to make it easier, or to get out of that chair there, or what kind of a house this house was, and who the people were in it. "Doesn't it ever snow in Rome?" he said.

"No," the girl said.

"Never?"

"If you like snow," she said, "you should go to Switzerland."

"I might at that," he said. "One thing about a war, you travel. Switzerland and snow. Have you been in Switzerland?"

"Before the war."

"I meant before the war," he said. "Nobody travels now but the armies. And that's no way to travel." Then, very carefully, he said: "What did Nina tell the Pulcinis? That I was your husband?"

"Yes."

"When were we married?"

"A year ago," she said. "In Naples."

"Oh." He paused. He was being funny. "Was it a nice wedding?"

"I don't know," the girl said. "I wasn't there."

He put the musette bag on the table. He would have preferred going into whatever room it was she had arranged in this house. He supposed there was a room; Nina had said there would be a room. But the girl did not move away from the table. "Do you have a family?" he asked then.

"My father."

"In Rome?"

"No; in Genoa," she said. He had, then, briefly a feeling of being glad that there was nobody. There being nobody seemed to make it simpler, although he did not know why he should want it simple. "You bombed Genoa," she said, "and my father thought I would be safer in Rome."

"Me?" he said. "I didn't bomb Genoa."

"Your countrymen."

"Oh." He looked at her, but he did not want to accept what looked like antagonism and trouble. She was so much prettier than he had expected. Her prettiness excited him. He did not want any trouble at all. It was to be very simple: a musette bag, and the room arranged for, and whatever money would be required.

"Genoa's in the north, isn't it?" he said. "Where Columbus came from."

"Yes."

"He used to sit on the dock and look out at the sea." He remembered that from a history book. "I haven't been in Europe before," he said. "I haven't been any place before. I grew up when Americans didn't think it was patriotic to travel to Europe. Europe was degenerate. A good American stayed home and discovered the beauties of Buffalo."

"Buffalo?" she said. "But that is an American animal."

"It was," he said. "Now it's just an American city."

"America is so rich," she said.

"The country is," he said.

"Are you?"

"Am I what?"

"Rich."

"No, I'm one of the poor ones." He smiled. "Are you disappointed?"

"I? No. Why should I be?"

"I thought Nina might have said I was one of the rich ones." Perhaps he should have boasted he was. The boys always said they were. The idea was to make them think you were even if you weren't. That made it easier, too, when they thought you were rich. And, of course, the point was to make it as easy as possible, and not to waste too much time talking. Just talk to them enough to make it easy.

She said: "Do you like Italy?"

It was the second time since he had entered the house he had been asked that. They obviously wanted you to like it.

"There's a lot of churches," he said.

"America has many churches too, hasn't it?"

"Yes," he said, "but we scatter them more."

"St. Paul's is very beautiful," she said. "People come from all over the world to see the cloisters at St. Paul's."

"Well, St. Paul's . . ."

"Don't you like St. Paul's?"

"Oh, I like it," he said. "But nothing happens to me when I see it. I mean I look at it and there it is: a church. How old are you?"

"Why?"

"I've been standing here trying to guess. Are you twenty-three?"

"It doesn't matter, does it?"

"No, it doesn't matter." He fumbled with the straps of the musette bag. "Two things surprised me," he said. "You're blonde and you're pretty."

"Should I have been dark and ugly?" she said.

"No," he said, "but I just didn't think you'd be that pretty." Then, pretending that he was interested in the musette bag, and not looking at her, he said: "Do you know many soldiers?"

She did not answer for a while, and when she did, her voice had changed. "What do you mean?"

"Nothing," he said, "but there are so many soldiers in Rome."

"Are there?" she said.

"A lot of the girls," he said, "like the soldiers."

"How fortunate," she said, "for the soldiers."

"Well," he said, "a lot of them do."

It was, of course, he realized, the wrong thing to have said, or at least it had been said much too soon, it was not something to have said at that particular moment or place, and he should have waited. He could feel that the hostility was back again in the room, and he was glad when the Signora Adele came back, smiling at them, and somewhat surprised to see them still there in the dining room.

"Oh," she said, "I forgot. Nina did not show you the room."

He realized, not knowing why, that the mention of the room only increased the look of aversion in her face, and yet, because she was here and because she was supposedly his wife there was hardly anything else she could do now except to get out of the chair finally and to follow Adele out of the dining room and into the hallway. He hefted the musette bag again, its bulky weight swinging against his hip, and went out, too, knowing something was wrong and not knowing what was wrong, or why it should be wrong. He carried the musette bag with him into the room at the end of the hallway. This was the room that had been arranged for. He could see that it was a rather large room, larger than he was accustomed to, with a high ceiling, and not too badly furnished, with a closet, a table, a fringed lamp on a small end table, and in the center of the room a big bed covered with a red smooth spread, and with red pillows propped against the headboard. It was unmistakably a room for two people, and one of them had to be a woman. And it was cold. It seemed much colder to him, as he stood there, easing the musette bag off his shoulder and on to the table, than the dining room had been. He wondered if Nina's captain had visited here, and what he had said about the coldness, and then what jokes were made about the best way to keep warm. Adele punched the pillows, and bustled around the room for a moment straightening things, and then she went out, closing the door. He was glad the musette bag was off his shoulder, because he had felt somewhat foolish carrying it about so constantly and, he imagined, so obviously.

Lisa stood in the center of the room, on the small rug, with her hands in her pockets, and looking at her he could not be certain he knew what she was thinking. He decided the thing for him to do was to ignore the hostility. He went and sat down now on the bed, thinking it was funny the spread should be that color. They could have chosen some other color. He blew on his hands. "It's cold," he said. "I'm shivering."

"Are your barracks warm?" she asked. She was being polite.

"Sure."

"Yes, the Americans manage to keep themselves warm."

He was supposed to apologize and feel guilty, too, about his warm barracks. They really weren't so goddam warm at that. "There's a big villa at Anzio," he said. "In the pine wood. Do you know it? I guess it belongs to some duke. The duke has quite a library. Or he had. He probably doesn't have it anymore."

"No? Why?"

"Oh, when I was there, there was a lieutenant in the library. The lieutenant was cold. He was feeding the duke's nice Latin manuscripts into a cozy fire."

"Yes?"

"Nothing. He was feeding them into the fire. He was cold."

"It must be wonderful," she said, standing there.

"What?"

"To be an American," she said, "and to be the conqueror of Europe."

He got up from the bed and went to the table where he had placed the musette bag. He began to unbuckle the straps. "It's all right," he said.

"Wherever you go," she said, "flowers, and the people cheering. You are the liberatori. And drinking wine. And then the girls, every place."

He opened the bag.

"I missed a couple of places," he said.

"Did you know girls in Africa?" she said.

"Yes, I knew girls in Africa."

"In Naples?"

"Yes, in Naples."

"Where else?"

"Caserta."

He took a can of milk out of the musette bag, and then some chocolate bars. He had talked the mess sergeant out of the can of milk, and the chocolate bars had been accumulated from his weekly rations. He had had no use for them before, except for some kids who used to come down and stand behind the barbed-wire fence, looking in, and then there were so many kids it was easier to give them the hard candy which hadn't much of a trading value anyway. He heard her, behind him, as he took the things out of the musette bag, say: "I think the Americans are liars."

He put the chocolate and the milk on the table.

"Why do you say they're liars?" he said.

"They make many promises. But they don't keep them."

"Depends on the promise."

"I think they are stupid, too," she said.

"Oh," he said, "we're a little bit of everything." He had taken a fruit cake, wrapped in its transoceanic cellophane, out of the bag. He held the cake up. "Do you like fruit cake?" he said. "My mother keeps sending me fruit cake and I hate it."

"What does your fiancée send you?"

She was ignoring the cake.

"My what?" he said.

"Your fiancée."

"She neglects me," he said.

"Does she?"

"Well," he said, "if I had one, she'd neglect me."

But she was refusing to look at the cake. She did not, obviously, think he was funny. He thought he was being funny, and he thought too that what he was doing was, as near as he could make it, kind. She stood there, in the raincoat, on the rug, not looking at the bed or the color of it or at anything in the room.

"I think the people despise you," she said.

"Do they?"

"You are arrogant and loud and stupid, and they despise you."

He put the cake down slowly. He had had great hopes about the influence of the cake.

"It's pretty hard despising a Sherman tank," he said.

"The conquistatori!" she said.

"Baby," he said, "it's better than being defeated."

"Italy is not defeated," she said.

"No? She's giving a pretty good imitation of it." Then he tried once more with the cake. He had really depended a great deal upon the cake. He held it up again, in its cellophane wraper. "Wouldn't you like to try my mother's fruit cake?" he said.

"Italy has been invaded by barbarians before," she said.

So it was hopeless, even with the cake.

"By what?" he said.

"Barbarians!"

"Now I'm a barbarian." The barbarian thing annoyed him. There was no reason it should have, more than the being stupid or arrogant or untrustworthy, but it did. "Look," he said, "you may have Leonardo da Vinci, but we've got U.S. Steel . . ."

"And it rusts," she said.

"And Da Vinci peels . . ."

"It lasts longer than metal!"

"But it ain't so hot on a tank," he said. He was almost angry now. He hadn't come here through the cold and the dark to have a political quarrel. But perhaps she could still be placated. He tried again. "How about some chocolate?" he said. "Wouldn't you like some chocolate?"

"Why do the Americans boast so much?" she said.

"Why do the Italians complain so much?" he answered.

"We've suffered!"

"We didn't cause it," he said.

"You bombed our cities."

"The Germans were in them," he said.

"And now you," she said.

He looked at her. He had become an enemy. And yet, he was no enemy, certainly not hers, certainly not anyone's in this house, not now, after having come this distance and through this cold. And yet she accused him, or seemed to accuse him. He had packed a bag and he had brought food and he had walked across the bridge. "Be grateful," he said, trying not to be angry. Not now, at least. "If we hadn't walked up here from Salerno," he said, "you'd still be doing the tedeschi's laundry . . ."

"Perhaps," she said, "it would have been better!"

"Would it?"

"Yes!"

"I'll invite the Jerries back," he said, being ugly about it now.

"We don't want either of you," she said.

"No?"

"No!" she said.

"Perhaps it was easier," he said, "sleeping with a kraut . . ."

"That's a lie!" the girl said.

"Don't tell me," he said, "you ate bananas out of the banana trees while the Jerries were here."

"We fought them," she said, furiously, "we fought them!"

"Where?" he said. "In bed?"

She came across the room to where he stood, holding the bar of chocolate, and she slapped him, and not thinking, feeling the cold impact of her hand on his check, he slapped her as quickly, and as he did so he could hear his own voice saying very evenly, not like his own voice at all, "Baby, I told you: you lost this war."

She turned and went toward the door of the bedroom. The bar of chocolate had broken in his hand. He already regretted slapping her. He tried to stop her. He did not want her to go. More than anything else now, he did not want her to go out of this room.

"Where are you going?"

He had put his back against the door.

She tried to get by him, and to open the door.

"There's nothing outside," he said.

"Let me go, please."

"But there's nothing outside," he said. He did not move away from the door. "God, you Italians have a temper," he said. "Do you always blow a fuse like that?"

The lights in the bedroom began to flicker. The lamp with the fringed shade on the small table next to the bed and the lamp on the table where he had placed his musette bag dimmed and grew bright and dimmed again. "I think," he said to the struggling girl, "we're having powerhouse trouble again. Why don't you people get your city fixed up?"

"Ask Admiral Stone!" she said.

"You don't happen to have a candle, do you?" he said.

"No!"

"Well, we're going to need one," he said, and the lights went down and faded out, and they were in darkness. In coldness and in darkness, like all the city.

She had moved away from him in the darkness. She was somewhere in the room. He could not tell where she was. He was afraid to abandon the door. The sense of being lost increased. He could feel the darkness changing him. Outside, in the hallway, he could hear the old man's voice. Ugo was calling, "Adele, the lights!"

"Sì, sì, I know," Adele answered. He could hear her voice. They were all excited and confused. "I am bringing a candle. Madonna, what a life!"

"Signor Roberto!" the old man called.

He shouted back: "The lights are out here too!"

"Eh, Madonna! Scusi," the old man said, as though he were responsible for the failure of the power. "I will bring a candle." He could hear them in the hallway moving about looking for candles and for matches.

"Lisa," he said, into the darkness.

There was no answer.

He could hear the sound of his own cold breathing.

"I'm sorry about the slap," he said, into the darkness.

She did not answer.

"Lisa," he said, "can you hear me? I'm sorry. And it's not true. About the girls, I mean."

She was somewhere there, in the darkness.

"It's been a long time," he said. "A long time since I've been with a girl. And I'm not your enemy."

Through the crack in the door a light flickered. He turned and opened the door. She could escape now if she wanted to. In the hallway, Ugo's thin face and almost bald head appeared lit by two wax candles. "Eh," the old man said, "the war, the war. Every day something else happens."

"That's all right," Robert said. "I like candles."

He took one of the wax tapers from the old man.

"It's usually only for a short time," Ugo said. "Then they repair it."

"We'll be all right," Robert said.

The old man made a gesture with his hands.

"Scusi," he said, apologizing again for the condition of his city, and then he went down the hall carrying his own candle, throwing a large and unhappy shadow.

Robert carried the candle into the room and put it on the table beside the musette bag and the small green can of milk and the chocolate bars. He was now a little ashamed of the bars of chocolate and the milk and the musette bag. When he had the candle adjusted, he turned to look at her. She was standing beside the bed that had that too obvious color. "Why don't you sit down?" he said. She stood there, in her raincoat, her chin down. The bedroom door was open. He picked out a package from the depths of the musette bag. "Oh," he said, "do you know what this is?" He showed her the package. "Soup," he said. "You wouldn't think they could put soup into a little package like this and send it all the way across the ocean and it would still be soup. But it is. All you have to do with it is put it into a pot of water and boil it five minutes and there it is—soup. My mother sent it."

The tinfoil sealed package was in his hand.

He watched her head lift slowly. Her hair was that very soft-looking blonde again in the light of the candle, and her shadow lay across the bed and on the wall.

"In such a small package?" she said.

"Sure."

His hands were cold and he had forgotten how cold he was and now he blew again on his hands. He took out his knife. It was a decorated knife he had bought from a wireman coming over on the boat. "Wouldn't you like me to cut you a piece of the fruit cake?" he said. She did not answer and he took the knife and cut through the cellophane and the cake. "Please," he said, holding the cake out.

"Grazie," she said.

She took the cake.

"Taste it," he said. "It's real good. I don't like cake but when my mother sends something it's pretty good."

He watched her taste the cake.

"Isn't it good?" he said, eagerly.

"Yes," she said. "Buonissimo."

"It came all the way from America," Robert said, watching her eat the cake.

4

B
ut it was no good. In the days that followed he was soon aware that the thing between them was no good. The weather stayed cold, and the governmental crisis continued, and the people burned charcoal, and the soldiers continued to come into the city on leave. The soldiers got drunk and the people hungrier, and that was about the only feature of life which had a certain constancy in those days. He tried not to think about or to accept the fact that it was no good between them. The night he had gone to bed with her, the first night, when she had at last accepted the fruit cake almost like a flag of truce, he had thought it might actually work out. He had sat finally on the edge of the bed. He said to her, "I have to be in camp at seven-thirty in the morning. Will you tell the signora to knock at the door in the morning?"

"Yes," she said.

And that was almost matrimonial, too, her saying the yes. She had gone out of the room then. He sat there, on the bed, unbuckling his boots, thinking how heavy and awkward they were, putting them carefully and noiselessly beside the bed. It was a very married gesture. The bed was frozen but the sheets were clean and he lay on the icy pillow, waiting for his own warmth to warm the bed, and for her return.

It was a real pillow. That was what impressed him most that first night. In Piombino, a town north of the city, he had been in a house. It was a ruined house and there had been an orchard outside. An orchard of fig trees and peach trees and there had been some grapes growing in an arbor and there had been a vegetable patch with tomato vines. It was a week he had eaten more tomatoes than he ever had in his life. He put the tomatoes in the sun and let them ripen and they were wonderful. The sea had been visible, too, from the top of the main street of the town and there was a little island that turned out to be Elba in the bay, blue, misty and unapproachable. The pillow in that house had been his raincoat under the blanket. But this was a real pillow, and clean.

He would have liked to have been casual and funny and to have said perhaps, "Come on, warm the bed up," but he did not say it. It was because he was hoping that nothing would damage the very temporary truce between them.

He lay there in the cold clean darkness.

He could hear her undressing in that darkness. She was standing on the small rug next to the bed, undressing, and as he lay there he listened to and followed the sounds of her clothes.

She must be shivering, he thought.

Once on a road in the south when he was marching, there had been an oxcart. Oxen, slow, white, sacrificial. And the wooden cart, driven by an old man in a black hat. The heat, the green fields of early summer. It was near a village where the Madonna in a roadside shrine had been broken by a shell. And on the back of the creaking and slow-moving cart, on the hay in the cart, there had been a woman. Young. And the strong brown naked legs and the naked shoeless feet under the black full-aproned skirt. That, and her smile. In that brown strong beautiful face, that smile. In the heat, during the marching. Coming back into the area, after the twenty miles they had marched, and after passing the light British tanks with their regimental pennants and their drivers, goggled, dusty, and in crash helmets, leaning out from the turrets between their machine guns, he remembered that smile. Its whiteness.

There had been, of course, the whores. And he had tried. He drove up, in the carriage they had hired, to the end of town, and outside the white stone peasant house there was a line of soldiers. They were very patient. The sun was hot, and the heat came up from the dust, and they squatted down on their heels in that line, waiting. There were two women in the white stone peasant house. The line moved about every ten minutes closer to the house and everybody was very patient, waiting in the dust and the sun, for the line to move up, like a chow line, and while they waited they squatted down on their heels and they smoked and then after about ten minutes the line moved up one man and they moved up with it and then they squatted down again, smoking and waiting. Even all the cognac he had in him at that time, and all the loneliness, had not been enough to get him to wait out that kind of line for what must have been at the end of it, and he walked back to town, and back to the bar near the Air Force club, and finished up the afternoon with cognac.

Now he could not stand the waiting.

He turned in the cold bed and found his matches on the small table and struck a match, the match flaring, cupping the light, and she stood there in the light of the held match for just a moment, her back toward him, looking at him over her shoulder, startled, for only a moment, then he blew the match out.

In the darkness he said, "Christ, you are beautiful," and that image held for him, the image of her turning to look at him over her naked shoulder in the light of the held match, and what Nina had said was perfectly true, she did have wonderful shoulders, and in that very short flickering moment in which he had held the match to see her she had been more beautiful than any girl he could remember.

Touching her, then, that first time, there had been no words at all to express the overwhelming sense of a woman being with him, in a clean place, in a clean bed, just being there, in a room, alone feeling the warmth even though it was not a given and voluntary and loving warmth, only the inevitable warmth of somebody's body. There were no words at all for the enormous charity that having a woman, in a room with a closed door, in a bed that was one's own, meant. He touched her with a quality of wonder and thankfulness. She said nothing. She did not move. But it was not necessary for her to say anything or even to give him anything. It was just the tremendousness of her being there. And he could not tell her that.

He fell asleep.

When she awoke in the morning he was gone. The moment of awakening was not at first one of panic. She was warm, and she did not remember immediately where she was, or what this room was, and then, when she did remember, and the panic began, there was the bad moment when, shivering and in haste, rising from the bed, she confronted her own accidental image in the long narrow mirror that was fixed to the door of the wardrobe closet. It seemed to her then that the thing she had done was incredible, that it had not been done by her at all, but by some unhappy and debased stranger, and then, on the table, she found the food he had so solicitously left behind for her, the milk, the chocolate, the soup package, coffee, even cigarettes, and she looked at the nakedness of the gifts as though they contained some terrible confirmation of the fact that the woman who had inhabited this room through the night had, after all, not been a stranger. She dressed quickly. She thought now that if she escaped quickly enough, if she went out quickly enough from this room, she would be able to leave behind that image the mirror had seen of the woman rising from the bed, and which only the mirror contained. She thought that once she had done this she would be able to escape quickly and forever because now she was being forced to escape, and she thought that when she had dressed she would go quickly somewhere, she did not know quite where, into the city she thought, and then somehow she would find something, work or something, somewhere, because she had to, now she had to more than ever, and then this room and the mirror and the food and the night would stop existing.

And she must, she thought, in the cold of the morning, get out of the room immediately the things he had left behind on the table so nakedly. She dressed herself in what she had worn the night before: the thick ski stockings, the heavy tasseled shoes, the woolen skirt, the woolen sweater. She put on her raincoat, not thinking that seeing her like this whoever was awake in the house would look perhaps strangely at her, and then going to the table she gathered up the gifts and went out of the room, carrying them down the hallway to the kitchen where she could hear sound and movement. Adele was standing at the stove, frying something in oil, the inevitabile cigarette in her mouth, and Antonio was sitting at the kitchen table. She heard Adele's "Good morning," and she went into the kitchen, and put the things he had left her, the mementoes, his part of the arrangement, on the kitchen table, and she said, "Will you take this, signora? There is too much—" and Adele was pleased. "Milk," she said, "and coffee. Guarda; chocolate, too. What is this?" She held up the sealed tinfoil package.

"Soup," Lisa said.

"Soup?" The astonishment was, perhaps, similar to her own. "But how? In a package?"

"It is dried soup."

"Un altro miracolo," Adele said. "They put everything in packages." She shook the tinfoil. "Well, one can't die from it." She looked at the girl. "Sit down, signora. Have some coffee."

"No, grazie."

"The coffee's ready." Reluctantly, Lisa sat down.

"Did you sleep well? Did the room please your husband?"

"Yes."

"In the old days, I wouldn't have thought of renting a room. But now . . ." She poured the coffee. "This is the last of Nina's captain."

"Good," Antonio said.

"Why? Good we had the coffee. You drink it."

"Reluctantly," Antonio said.

"Nevertheless, you drink it," Adele said.

Antonio smiled across the table at her. "Do you know Leopardi, signora?"

"Leopardi?" Lisa said. "The poems?"

"Yes."

"No. I know very little poetry."

"'O patria mia,'" Antonio quoted, "'I see the walls and the arches and the columns and the images and the heraldic shields of our ancestors, but the glory I do not see.'"

His smile made her uncomfortable. "'But the glory I don't see,'" Antonio said, repeating his Leopardi. "'Their coffee I see." He stirred his cup. "Signor Roberto is a private, isn't he?"

"Yes," the girl said.

"Antonio means," Adele said, "that in our army he was an officer. That is something to boast about."

"I am not boasting," Antonio said. "It doesn't matter what I was. What I was exists only in the Libyan desert. I only meant a girl like you, signora, might have married one of their officers."

She flushed.

"Was I unfortunate?"

"No," Antonio said. "I suppose their privates are richer than our colonels. What does your husband do, signora—in America?"

"In America?" she said.

"Yes. When he is a civilian. Where the war is over."

"He is studying to be a lawyer," Lisa said.

"An avvocato? Very good," Adele said.

I am lying, Lisa thought; why should I be? Why do I try to make him somebody or something important? Perhaps he works in a garage. Perhaps he is nothing.

"A lawyer?" Antonio said, politely. "He does not look like a lawyer. But then, even their priests—have you seen their priests?—they don't look like priests either. Their priests look like soccer players."

"The military ones," Adele said.

"Do we ever see anything but their military ones?" Antonio said. He stood up. "'Ma la gloria non vedo,'" he said, again quoting Leopardi. "Do you know, signora, when I left in my transport from Augusta to sail for Africa there was a time when I thought I would enjoy the war? I thought it would force me into a heroism, and to be a hero, even a reluctant one, is an attractive idea. I thought war was something like fire-fighting: a great blaze, and then men, all together, working to put it out." He grinned, savagely, and she realized that the mockery was not directed at her, but at himself, at that poor illusioned Antonio who had gone into the transport at Augusta. "But how wrong I was; war is the opposite of men working together. It is more than ever only men trying to save themselves separately. At Bardia I was cured of being a fool about war forever."

"And now?" Lisa said.

"Now?" He looked intently at her. He hesitated. "Excuse me, signora—but your husband, have you found it possible to be happy with a," and there was again that slight pause as he chose the word, "stranger?"

"A stranger?" Lisa said. "But all men are strangers."

"I meant a foreigner, an American."

"They are generous," she said, "and not all of them are alike."

"Have you been happy?"

She did not answer.

"Excuse me," Antonio said. "Perhaps I should not ask. But it is difficult for me to accept certain things."

"That our women marry foreigners?"

"No," Antonio said. "That they don't marry them. That they sell themselves to them."

She stood up, abruptly. It was absolutely necessary to escape, and to escape now, this moment, while she could. "Excuse me," she said. She went out of the kitchen and then out of the house. The grayness of winter inhabited everything: sky, building, street. And it seemed to her, walking rapidly, with the cold coming through the inadequate raincoat she wore, that almost all of the faces of the young men she passed were like Antonio's, and she thought how similar their memories (of transports, defeat, the desert) must be. Her own urgency had increased now; she had already lied, saying he was a lawyer, defending him, involving herself deeper, when what she wished above all was to end it, to close off forever the house, the room, and the night. She walked quickly down the Via Flaminia toward the city. A truck, one of her countrymen's, going down the wide boulevard exploded from a protruding exhaust pipe a dense black cloud of something that was hardly gasoline. Near the old enormous stone gate, whose archways led into the Piazza del Popolo, a starved cabman's horse stamped, his ribs covered with a soldier's blanket. At the trolley terminal, a clump of people waited with that incredible patience born out of the war and disaster for the infrequent circolare.

She crossed the dung-spotted cobbles, under the archways, avoiding the horn blasts of the vehicles, passing on her left the old church Nero's ghost was supposed to haunt, the city's birds roosting on its stone, and then the piazza itself, wide, with the fountain and obelisk in its geometrical center, and the park above it, and the statuary at each side. Three avenues fanned out from the piazza, and she walked toward the central one, the Corso. He sat on the edge of the bed, she remembered, unbuckling his boots, and in the darkness there had been that intensified and unrelaxed waiting, that expectation of his hands, and she remembered too, shrinkingly, that when he had touched her, later, something in her had not been entirely unwilling.

She hurried on; a café, a tobacco shop, a store that once sold lingerie, the department stores with bare windows; it was the hotel she wanted, thinking this would be preferable, and thinking that the French would be different, not knowing why, thinking a hotel run by the French would be differently run than one by the Americans or the English. There were two sentries, short and swarthy, in white helmets and white leggings, outside the hotel; they did not salute her as she went through the revolving door. At the desk, in the lobby, she did not know quite how to ask; where could one find the military manager? The clerk, a countryman, as the elevator boys and the waiters and the men who take care of the lavatory were countrymen, looked at her, and then indicated a door beyond the desk and behind him. The office was paneled; there was a window the length of the wall; the desk was glasstopped and of some polished black wood; the Frenchman was a major. She sat in a leather-upholstered chair. I must smile, she thought; I'm not smiling. How could she explain how necessary the work was to her, and yet smile? The major sat, swiveling slowly in the chair, talking of Siena. Did the signorina know Siena?

"Yes," Lisa said.

"A beautiful city. I like cities," the major said, with old walls around them. We occupied it once, I think. In the sixteenth century. I was very fond of the Duomo. And the Pinturicchios. Have you been to the Pinturicchios, signorina?"

"No," Lisa said. "I know very little about art."

"Oh, it wasn't the art," the major said. "I was more astonished at the real gold and the jewels they used than at the paintings. Actual gold." He spun a little in his comfortable chair. "So you like to work."

"Yes," Lisa said.

"Well, one can always use another secretary. Are you married, signorina?"

She hesitated; but why? Why should she hesitate?

"No," she said.

"Good," the major said. "Marriage is such an inconvenience. One must always be home at a certain hour. But with no husband—one is independent. I prefer independence. Do you, signorina?"

"Yes," Lisa said.

"So," the major said. "Work. There are many girls who come into the hotel for work. Some of them type. Some take shorthand. Some lack those simple talents. Do you type, signorina?"

"No."

"Or take shorthand?"

"No."

"Oh," the major said. "Neither. Well. What can you do?"

"Perhaps answer the telephone," Lisa said. "Anything."

"Anything," the major said. "That's interesting.

"What is the anything you would be willing to do?"

She did not answer.

"There are few jobs, and many girls," the major said. "They come in all day. Each is anxious. Well, one should take the most anxious, and the most independent, no?"

She stood up, fingering her purse, and the major leaned back in the swivel chair.

"We are not that independent, are we, signorina?"

"No."

"Well," the major said. "Buon giorno."

"Buon giorno," she said.

Outside, the clerk, her countryman, avoided looking at her,

and the sentries stamped, snapping their arms, as the revolving door turned.

Che bestie! she thought: che bestie! And now the French were included.

So that was no escape, and yet she could not accept the other thing: the waiting in the room for evening to come, in the room, and hearing him enter the house, hearing him say buona sera to Adele or to Mimi or to Ugo when he entered, bringing, as she knew he would, because that was his part of the arrangement and he kept to it scrupulously, the musette bag, and what was in the musette bag. And always, when he entered, the first few days, there was the formality of the greeting, and it was always the same, she sitting on the bed, pretending to read sometimes, or pretending to sew, and Robert blowing on his hands, saying how cold it was, and she would say yes, wasn't it cold, and then he would say yes, certainly was cold.

They went out the second evening because Robert wanted to, and sat in a little neighborhood café, and he drank vermouth, the ice floating in the glass, and she had a gelato, with a small flavored lozenge on top which dripped a fruit brandy down into the richness of the cream, and the night they went there was an incident at the bar. There were always incidents. At the bar, the night they were there, the second night they were together, there was a Negro soldier, drinking cognac, dressed in a thick parka, and she sat, listening to them, the Negro and the proprietor, talking. She watched the teeth of the Negro: how enormous they were, how white. And the voice: how differently they all spoke, in some the speech nasal and grating, in some the speech thick and rich, and the tongue and the teeth were used a great deal when they spoke. All the tables had been taken indoors during the winter, and the chestnut trees outside the café were stripped and bare. But in the summer the strolling musicians would come. It was the Negro talking that had made her think of the musicians in the summertime. Then as she watched she realized the Negro was selling, in his musical speech that made her think of the strolling musicians, or was about to sell cigarettes to the proprietor, and all the music, of both languages, was concerned only with the price of the cigarettes. Then she watched the Negro with the musical speech take from inside his thick hooded parka a carton of cigarettes, and the proprietor went to his cash register and rang up a no-sale and took his money out of the register and gave it to the Negro who, flashing those splendid teeth, smiled and finished his cognac and went out of the café, and right after that there was the incident. The incident consisted of the proprietor tearing off the wax-paper covering of the carton of cigarettes, and tearing open the cardboard, and then tearing open a package of cigarettes, and there were no cigarettes at all in the package, there was straw or dung or whatever the Negro soldier had been able to find and roll cigarettes of that would feel enough like cigarettes in the carton, and the proprietor, swearing and calling down maledictions upon the heads of all the armies, especially the Ethiopian one, ran out of the café into the cold, wildly looking about for the musical voice, and Robert had laughed, and they left the café soon afterward.

Then they were back again in the room, for everything that happened between them of any importance revolved about the room. In the newspaper there was a funny cartoon, and lying on the bed she laughed at the cartoon. The newspaper was spread out on the red cover of the bed. The cartoon was a political one and showed Romulus and Remus and they had just completed cutting that long furrow within which Rome was to be built according to the legend. They were lying under a tree, resting, and the plowshare was still deep in the earth beside them. Then Romulus said to Remus: Now that we have completed building a city where the Alleati can have a good time, let us build one for ourselves.

She laughed because it was so true and so funny, and they had just come from the café.

"It's not that funny," Robert said.

"No?" she said. "You laughed at the cigarettes."

"Well, that was pretty funny. When he opened up the carton."

"But the man paid for them."

"Well, the jig paid for his cognac, and that wasn't real either."

"Jig?"

"The Negro."

"It is not funny to pay two thousand lire for cigarettes and then find only straw."

He had brought now, the second night, an alarm clock with him, and he had taken the alarm clock out of his musette bag, and as he did so she thought of him coming like this every night with that bag as a miner might come home after work with a pickax or a lawyer with a briefcase. He was winding the alarm clock.

"I brought the clock so that Adele won't have to knock on the door in the morning," he said.

He put the clock on the end table near the bed.

"That looks very domestic," he said, looking at the clock.

She did not answer.

"It's almost like I had to go to work in the morning. Would you mind if I left my raincoat here? Just in case it rains."

"If you wish."

"I'll hang it in the closet."

He opened the door of the wardrobe closet. Only her raincoat was hanging in the closet on a hanger, and below the raincoat there was a valise, with all the valise straps buckled. He hung his raincoat in the closet, beside hers, and he knew then because of the valise that nothing was really settled yet. Despite the alarm clock.

"Do you know," he said, "I was afraid when I came tonight that you might not be here."

"Were you?"

"Yes," Robert said. "I thought the room might be empty. I thought I'd come and there would be nobody here but the Pulcinis and some excuse."

"What would you have done?"

She was pretending to read the newspaper.

"I don't know."

"You would have found another one," Lisa said. "There are other girls in the city."

The clock ticked, matrimonially.

"Thousands of them," Robert said. "Aren't you cold in that raincoat?"

"I'm accustomed to it."

He had bought a bottle of vermouth in the wineshop in the neighborhood. He opened the vermouth, at the table, while she lay there with the newspaper spread out on the bed, and the clock ticked. "Is the valise in the closet yours?"

"Yes."

"Why don't you unpack it?"

She did not answer. He poured the vermouth, liking the color of the wine, into a glass. "What did you do with the stuff I left here this morning?"

"Your gifts?"

"They weren't gifts. They were just things I left for you."

"I gave them to Adele."

"Oh." He drank the vermouth. "You were sleeping when I woke up. You were all cuddled up. You looked cute."

"Cute?"

"Carina," Robert said. "We say cute."

"Cute," the girl said, pronouncing it. "What words they use for endearments. Babbee, darling, cute. What a language for love. Everything is said with the teeth. The, the—" she said, showing him how the tongue had to click against her teeth in order to say it.

"The," Robert said, repeating it. "It doesn't sound hard to me."

"Italian is soft," she said, "and musical. And the language says exactly what it means. The," she said again, contemptuously. "What is it? Masculine? Feminine?"

"It's neuter," Robert said.

"The," she said. "In Italian nothing is neuter. The article agrees with the noun. Masculine or feminine."

"That's fine," Robert said. "I like that. I don't think things should be neuter either."

"I mean the language," she said.

"I don't," he said. "I mean everything."

He came across the room, and sat down beside her, and folded the newspaper she had been reading. "I'm glad you didn't go away," he said. "I'm glad you were here when I came tonight." She did not answer. "I was," he hesitated over the word a little, "pretty happy last night."

"Grazie," the girl said. "I'm glad you were pleased."

"Weren't you?"

She shrugged.

"Non importa," she said. She looked away. "Why did you light the match?"

"Last night?"

"Yes."

"To look at you."

"Why?"

"Because you're beautiful."

"I don't like it," she said. "I'm not an animal in a stable you come to look at in the night. To admire because you own it. To see if it's comfortable."

"I didn't mean it like that."

She picked at the edge of the pillow. "Antonio asked me today what you do in America."

"What did you say?"

"That you were studying to be a lawyer."

"Who, me? I'm no lawyer. I'm not even an engineer. I used to work for a newspaper."

"A journalist?" she said, hopefully.

"No," Robert said. "Not even a journalist. I used to sell ads. Advertisements. Like these." He indicated the advertisements in the newspaper she had been reading. "That isn't much to boast of to Antonio, is it?" He smiled at her. "What are you thinking?"

"Nothing."

"Would you have liked me to be an officer and a lawyer?"

"Non importa," the girl said.

"You always say that."

"What?"

"Non importa."

She shrugged again. "But nothing is," she said. "You are not a lawyer, I am not a prima ballerina."

"No," Robert said, "we're only like the two things in your language: masculine and feminine. Do you go to church Sunday?"

"No. Why do you ask?"

"I thought you might like to go to Lake Bracciano. I could get a jeep from my company. Would you like to go? If you don't go to church, that is."

"I have nothing to go to church for."

"Well, people go to pray."

"I'm in anger with God."

The phrase amused him. "All right. We'll go to Bracciano. You're not in anger with Lake Bracciano, are you?" He looked at her, wishing he could feel safe enough or sure enough of her to touch her. He wanted very much to touch her now. "One of the boys in my company is in love with a girl. An Italian girl. He's married. But he's going home and he's going to get divorced and then he's coming back for her."

"And she believes him?" Lisa said.

"Sure."

"What a fool. He'll never come back."

"He might. Boats go both ways. And he says he will."

"He won't," Lisa said. "He'll use her and that will be all."

"You don't trust anybody, do you?" Robert said. "You don't think anybody keeps a promise."

"Words don't make flour," she said.

"What's that? A proverb?"

"Yes."

"You seem to know a lot about men and their promises."

"Yes," she said. "You know how experienced we Italians are."

"How many men have you known?"

"Hundreds."

"I wouldn't be surprised."

"Of course," she said. "I have a different one in every city. Rich, too. Doctors, lawyers, engineers. That's why I'm here in this room with you. Because I know so many men and I've had so many lovers."

He put his glass down beside the alarm clock. The clock ticked; and he had set the alarm for seven-thirty. "Do you have a proverb about happiness?"

"Only that God sends flies to the starved horse."

"How about a proverb about how happiness doesn't gather moss or something? Don't you have a proverb like that?"

"No."

"Too bad. Happiness isn't neuter. How's that for a proverb?"

"You're drunk," she said.

"I'm not drunk," he said. "I just feel good. Do you mind? I feel good because I'm in a room. With four walls, and a door. It's wonderful. You can close the door. You can lock it. And besides, you didn't run away. I thought you might. But you didn't. I always thought that when I would finally be in a room with four walls and a door you could close I would go up to my girl and kiss her. Like this."

After a while, he took his mouth away. "Lisa," he said.

"Yes."

"Nothing. I just wanted to say your name."

She leaned back against the pillow and she was quiet. Then she said: "You are not even a lawyer."

"No," Robert said, "I'm not even a lawyer."

"You are nothing."

"Practically nothing," Robert said.

Then she said: "Will you go out for a moment?"

"Out of the room?"

"Yes."

"Why?"

"Please."

"All right," he said. He stood up. "I'll go smoke a cigarette." He went out of the room. Ugo was sitting in the dining room, reading. "Ah, Signor Roberto."

"What's the signor for?" Robert said.

"Va bene," Ugo said. "Roberto."

"What are you reading?"

"*Il Tempo.*"

He sat down at the table, and shook out two cigarettes. "I haven't read a real newspaper in two years. What's *Il Tempo* have to say?"

"The usual. The war will end soon: the war will not end soon. One has a choice."

"Oh, it'll end. Two things are always sure about a war: they begin and they end."

"Yes," Ugo said. "It's the time in between that nobody understands. How is your signora?"

"Fine."

"She's a fine girl," Ugo said. "I like her very much. She is the only girl who has been in this house my son Antonio has liked."

"That's a compliment," Robert said. "Antonio must be hard to please."

"I'm afraid he is."

"Well," Robert said, "what Antonio ought to do is fall in love. He's old enough."

"There was a girl once," Ugo said. "My son never talks of her now. You know, after the peace was signed, he deserted from the army—so as not to have to fight for the Germans. And I hid him."

"Hid him?"

"Yes," Ugo said. "It was necessary. For two months he was hidden in the cellar in this house . . ."

"And the girl?"

"She fell in love with a German." The old man paused: "She worked in the telephone exchange and when the Germans retreated she went north with them. So you see—there was the desertion, and then the girl—and now, well, what one has now. It has happened to all our sons . . . sometimes I think that whatever happens to us after the war, whatever happens to Italy, what we become, will all be because of the things that are happening to our young now . . . and they are not good things, Roberto: they are very bad. To have no work, to have no faith, to have nothing they can take pride in, to have nothing they really love . . . If the seedling is twisted, the whole tree grows crooked . . . and then, I myself don't understand things too well. Nothing has turned out like we expected . . . We thought that if the fascists were gone—well, the fascisti are gone, and now? Our own lives are small, and perhaps not too important. We thought that prison was one of the worst indignities one could suffer—now how simple the going to prison looks! I used to play cards in the cell . . ."

"What are you, Ugo?"

"A kind of socialist who is more of an old man than he is a socialist. You see, in Italy, we're always a kind of something.

Not the exact thing, like the Germans or the English. But only a kind of, with many shades."

"Oh," Robert said, "it's only because of the war. Afterward, you'll be all right."

"Well," the old man said, "we live in hope."

"Yes," Robert said. "What else is there to live in?" He stood up. "Good night."

"Buonanotte, Roberto."

He went out of the dining room.

The bedroom was dark. He closed the door, and groped his way in the darkness until he touched the side of the bed. "Lisa?" he said.

"Sì."

"Where are you?"

"Here."

"I can't see a thing," he said. He moved away from the bed in what he thought was the direction of the closet. When his hands touched it, he opened the closet door and took his jacket off, and reached into the darkness of the closet for a hanger, and as he did so he touched the dresses. Two dresses, he could feel, were hanging in the closet. Her dresses. Finally. He found a hanger, and hung his jacket away, in the closet, beside the dresses and the two raincoats.

"Lisa," he said, in the icy and clean feel of the bed linen.

"Yes."

"We'll go Sunday to Lake Bracciano. All right?"

"Va bene."

"What are you thinking about?"

"Niente."

"You're so quiet you must be thinking about something."

"About God," she said.

"God?"

"Yes," she said, in the darkness. "That He has a lot to forgive me, and I have as much to forgive Him."

So on Sunday, he took her for a drive to Lake Bracciano, thinking she would like it. The lake was to the north of the city and the Germans had retreated along this road. He had gotten the jeep, after a good deal of persuasion, out of the motor pool. It was a clear day, and he was proud of the fact that he had secured a jeep. He thought that taking her in the jeep was a way of showing her that she was really his girl and that he was taking her for a drive on a Sunday as he would if he were home and had a girl.

She sat on the hard canvas cushion of the jeep, and she must have felt exposed. The jeep had not been winterized. He didn't realize at first that she felt exposed.

They drove out of the city and down the road that went to Lake Bracciano. Now and then they passed an armored car or a tank, broken and stripped, lying in the fields, rust eating the guns and the axles. Because it was Sunday people were walking on the road. When the jeep went through the small towns the people moved reluctantly out of the roadway, and if they were young people they moved very reluctantly out of the way of the jeep, and everybody out strolling looked at her sitting in the car. If they were young they shouted. But he did not understand what they had shouted.

She turned quickly.

"Go back," she said.

"What?"

"I want to go back," she said. "Please."

"But we're halfway there. What's the matter?" he said. He looked at her. "What did they shout at you?"

"Nothing."

"They shouted something. What did they shout?"

"Nothing."

She did not speak again until they came to Lake Bracciano. There was an enormous castle dominating the little town above the lake. The town itself was built on the saddle of a hill and

the main street climbed steeply up to the castle, and it was difficult getting the jeep through the narrow streets, and in the
central piazza the men in their Sunday black and their old
black hats, smoking their thin strong cigars, turned and looked
at her sitting in the jeep, and they muttered something to themselves, too, about her. That was when he began to realize how
exposed she must feel. But he drove down to the lake, and it
lay, very blue and circular and beautiful, at the foot of the
mountains. There were small docks with rowboats tied up at
them. In the summer it would be even lovelier here. They sat
for a while, looking at the lake, and then, seeing a pensione, he
wanted to go into the pensione and get something to eat. She
did not want to go, but he insisted. It was a small hotel at
which people lived in the summertime. They sat down at a
table. A waiter came up to the table.

There was a sign on the wall that said BIRRA.

"Would you like something to eat?" he said to the girl.
"Maybe they have some spaghetti. Do you have any spaghetti?" he asked the waiter.

"No," the waiter said.

"Then how about some eggs? Do you have any eggs?"

"No," the waiter said.

He looked at the BIRRA sign.

"It says beer," he said to the waiter. "From Naples. Do you
have any beer?"

"That's a sign from before the war," the waiter said.

"Well, what can we have? Don't you have any food?"

"You have the food," the waiter said.

"What?"

"Please," the girl said, "I don't want anything."

They got up and went out of the hotel. They drove back
through the town, through the piazza, where the short square
men in black smoked their cigars, and past the castle, and
down the hill again to the road which went back to the city.

Going back, the fields and the small towns, with their painted stone houses, were not as pretty as he had thought them, and then, as they were driving, they passed an old lumbering truck on the road in the back of which there was a family. There was a small boy and a young girl and a woman in the back of the truck, and up front there was an old man and a middle-aged man was driving. The truck had no tires on the two rear wheels, and they were driving it on the bare rims, and the whole truck shook and wheezed, and the small boy was leaning over the side of the truck, shaking with it, as they drove past. When they were only a little way past the truck something hit him in the back of the head, and a bitten apple fell into his lap, and he put the brakes on, stopping the jeep abruptly. He got out and stood in the middle of the road and stopped the lumbering truck with its tormented rear wheels. He went back to where the family was, and he said, "Who threw that apple?"

The husband got down and came back to where he was standing. The husband looked at the jack he had carried with him out of the jeep.

"What is it?" the husband said.

"One of you threw an apple at me," he said. "I want to know who threw the apple."

The husband looked at him again, and turned to the boy and the young girl and the woman in the back of the truck. "Did you throw an apple?" he asked.

"I threw it," the small boy said.

"He did not mean to hit anything," the mother said. "He was throwing the apple away."

"Scusi," the husband said.

He walked back to the jeep, carrying the jack. Like hell he didn't mean to hit anything. He went through all the small towns fast on the way back to the city, and he didn't much care how pretty the countryside was. Or how lovely Lake Bracciano.

But that, and the other things, helped make it no good.

5.

New Year's Eve came. On New Year's Eve, the English sergeant was sitting again in the dining room, listening to the music on the radio. Because the music libraries of the army radio station were limited, they were still playing Christmas carols and alternating the Christmas carols with patriotic songs. The fact that it was New Year's Eve made the Englishman feel sadder than he had at any other time during the year. He had been six years in the army now, and it was a long time. Six years could make a man feel that he had never been in anything else than an army. He looked now at little Mimi, the Pulcini's maid, who was clearing up in the dining room, and he said, "How old are you, Mimi?"

"Sedici," the girl said.

"I've a gel in England most your age," the English sergeant said. "Want a piece of chawklit?"

"Sì."

"Like chawklit, do you?" She nodded her head. "Well, then, come along and give us a kiss for it."

"No, no," Mimi said. "Proibito."

"Who says a bit of a kiss is proibito?"

"Sì," Mimi said. "Alla signora dispiace."

"You tell the old hag to mind her business," the sergeant said. "Now, come on, give a chap one."

She giggled a little. She wore a holiday ribbon in her hair. She gave the sergeant a quick and birdlike kiss.

"There, that's better," the sergeant said, nodding his

cropped head. "Here's your chawklit. Mind, you don't eat it all at once now."

"Molte grazie," Mimi said.

"Well," the sergeant said, watching her devour the chocolate quickly, "it's tonight being New Year's Eve made me feel like havin' somebody kiss me."

"Sì, comincia domani il nuovo anno," Mimi said.

"Ay, it's a new year tomorrow all right," the sergeant said, "and they must be havin' a proper time for themselves tonight in Piccadilly Circus."

Ugo Pulcini came into the dining room. His spectacles sat up on his high forehead. "Buona sera," he said to the sergeant. The sergeant looked up at the old man. He thought Ugo a queer bloke. But decent enough. Always reading something, too. Bloke could go blind reading them Eyetie newspapers with their bad print. "'Ullo," the sergeant said. He gestured toward the wine bottle.

"Have a bit of vino?"

Little Mimi ducked out of the room. She worried briefly that the chocolate had stained her mouth. The signora did not like her accepting gifts from the soldiers.

"No, grazie," Ugo said, refusing the wine.

"Funny," the sergeant said, "how you blokes never drink the vino you sell us."

"But this," Ugo said, "is a vino dei castelli."

"Is it?"

"A good wine," Ugo said.

"Oh, vino's vino," the Englishman said. "Pop it into you, puke it out."

"Before the war," Ugo said, "you should have gone to Frascati. There was wonderful wine—famous!"

The Englishman poured wine into his own glass. He considered it, and possibly his own predicament. "You know," he said, "you're not such bad chaps, considerin', you Eyeties.

Bunch of excitable johns, though. Always full of the bellyache.
Always cheerin' a bloke or shootin' him."

Ugo smiled.

"There are many," he said, "we would like to shoot we will
not have the pleasure of shooting." Which was, of course,
regrettable. Even with the war, there had not been enough
shooting of the right kind. The windowpanes rattled. The Englishman sighed. He had small blue eyes, with a certain pleasant
dullness about them, the flesh about the corners of the eyes
deeply wrinkled. The desert sun might have done that. Ugo,
glancing up now, saw Robert in the door. Robert came into the
room. He was carrying a bottle of cognac.

"Did Lisa call?" he asked Ugo.

"No."

He is worried, Ugo thought. They were all worried. Except
the Englishman, perhaps. The English did not worry.

"Where did she go?" Robert said. "It's almost midnight. She
always waits for me to come from camp."

"There is nothing to worry about," Ugo said.

"In this city?" Robert said. He was restless. He put the bottle of cognac down on the table. Outside, it was New Year's
Eve, the last fading night of a vanishing sequence of nights,
and as dark as all the other nights in that sequence had been.
The streets were dangerous as well as dark and cold. He
looked at the old man sitting comfortably at the table.

"She'll be home soon," Ugo said.

Yes, Robert thought, she'll be home. The Englishman had
red hair on the backs of his short thick fingers. Home. That
was what he had wanted, hadn't he? An imitation of home.

"Take your king," the Englishman said. "Why kick up such
a bloody fuss about the old boy? It ain't bad, having a king."

"The House of Savoy has not been exactly a blessing for us,"
Ugo said.

"Well, we like having one," the Englishman said.

"Perhaps you can afford to," Ugo said.

Robert opened the bottle of cognac.

"Why," the Englishman said, "I've seen His Majesty, in the cinema, right in bombed Coventry, and there he was, talkin' to the poor duffers in their own homes. Cheerin' 'em up, and comfortin' 'em. Face to face."

"Yes?" Ugo said, politely.

"Gives 'em something to look up to," the sergeant said.

"Yes?" Ugo said. "I will tell you a story. There was once a woman who had three children. They were named Benito, Victor Emmanuel, and Italia. When she was asked why she had named them so, the woman answered: Because Benito eats all the time, Victor Emmanuel sleeps all the time . . . and Italia . . ."

Ugo paused.

"Italia," he said, "weeps all the time."

"Oh, mind you," the Englishman said, "I ain't saying I don't like you Eyeties."

"Of course not," Ugo said.

"It's a pretty country. 'Course, it's a bit dirty, and unmodern, and it ain't like being in England where a bloke knows what's what. But it's a bloody sight better'n Africa."

"Were you in Africa?" Ugo asked.

"Three damn bloody years," the sergeant said.

Robert drew a cigarette from his pack and gave it to the old man. He was trying not to think of her being in the streets, if she was in the streets. He did not know where she was. He realized that while he was in camp during the day he did not ever know where she was or what she did. And he did not know if he had a right to ask her, or how much right of any kind he had. The old man had taken the cigarette.

"In '43," Ugo said, "we smoked cigarettes made of roasted acorns."

"Acorns?" Robert said.

"Yes; truly. Acorns."

"How were they?"

"Impossible." The old man smiled. He paused.

"When ends the war, Roberto?"

Robert shrugged. "When the war ends."

"It is such a long one this time," the old man said. He thought of its length, and of its sadness. "In '14 it was a different war."

"Men died, didn't they?" Robert said.

"Of course."

"Then it isn't much different." He poured the cognac into a small glass beside Ugo's arm. He liked the old man. "Have some cognac, Ugo. I bought it to celebrate New Year's."

"Grazie," Ugo said.

"How about you, England?"

"No. Vino's fine for me, Yank."

Robert lifted his glass. "If you can still see out of one eye after you drink this, it's good cognac . . ."

Ugo tasted the liquor. His face puckered. "And you paid for it?" he said.

"Eight hundred lire . . ."

"The bottle?"

"What did you expect, the gallon?"

The old man shook his head. "This isn't cognac like we once had."

"They ain't lire like you once had either . . ."

Nothing was like what one once had had. The Englishman sucked on his pipe. "They must be havin' themselves a proper time tonight in Piccadilly Circus . . ."

"Do you wish to be home?" Ugo asked.

"Ay. I'd like to have a go at the missus again." He put the glass of wine down carefully. "She writes, the missus. Had a letter. She says: I don't know what you're eatin' tonight—ay, what I'm eatin'!—but what we're sittin' down to is codfish roes and potatoes. Codfish roes! She hates codfish roes, me missus."

He sucked mournfully on his pipe. He wondered if in Piccadilly Circus the night was as cold and as dark. Then he wondered if everywhere in the world it was as cold and as dark and as lonely as it was here.

Robert heard the door in the hallway open, and then her voice, low, talking to Adele. When she came into the dining room she was flushed with the cold, and her hair was blown about. She did not look at him as she came into the dining room. Adele followed her.

"Buona sera," she said.

"Is it cold out?" Ugo asked.

"Brutto," she said. "It is so dark one is almost afraid to walk alone."

"Our New Year's," Adele said.

Robert held his voice down. "Where have you been?" he asked her.

"A friend's," she said, not looking at him.

"She kept you sort of late, didn't she?" Robert said.

She did not answer.

"Yesterday, on the Lungotevere, they found a soldier," Ugo said, "Stripped naked . . . but completely!"

"Have some vino, ma'am," the Englishman said.

"No," Lisa said, "grazie."

Robert looked at his watch. "It's six o'clock in New York now. They're probably dressing for dinner. It's a big night."

"Bloody big night," the English sergeant said.

"While you are having such a dull night in Rome," the girl said.

"Just a night," Robert said.

Antonio, in the familiar raincoat, entered the room. He went to his mother and kissed her.

"If only the war would end," Ugo said.

"And when it ends?" Adele said.

"God pity Italy when it ends," Antonio said.

The Englishman looked into his wine glass. More than five years, and he hadn't seen his missus. Egypt, North Africa, the desert and the mountains, and the billets, double-decked, in some old warehouse or factory.

"Oh, you chaps are always complainin'," the Englishman said.

"Don't we have the right to complain?" Antonio said.

"You're always fightin' the bloody war," the Englishman said. "Give it a rest." Codfish roes, she hated them. And now the buzz bombs. A bloody mess, all of it.

"Have the English," Antonio said, "now forbidden us to speak?"

"How about some cognac, Antonio?" Robert said.

"Antonio . . ." Ugo said.

"I was playing billiards tonight," Antonio said, ignoring his father, "and an American came into the café. A lieutenant. He was with a girl."

"A signorina?" Adele said.

"Also an American. A woman in a uniform. They had been celebrating. He was teaching her to play billiards. Do they permit women into your billiard rooms in America?" he asked Robert.

"Well, there's no law keeping them out," Robert said.

"But do they frequent billiard rooms?"

"No."

"In Italy they feel free to," Antonio said. "It is very convenient to leave their morals behind, isn't it, signor? In her own country she would feel too much shame to enter a café and play billiards in a room where there were only men. But not in Italy. One does not feel shame before an inferior people. So it is nothing to come into a place like that, a little drunk, and lean over a table, and laugh very loudly, with her skirt up to here, and to have a good time. After all, who will object—those dirty Italians standing silently against the wall? She enjoyed herself . . ."

"Eh," Adele said, "it's not that important."

"No?" Antonio said.

"Of course," Adele said, "I wouldn't go. But if she wants to, and she doesn't mind . . ."

"They have already taken over our houses," Antonio said. "Our hotels. Our stadiums. Our restaurants. And now, our billiard rooms."

He turned to the Englishman:

"Shall we shut our mouths entirely?"

On the walls of the small villages in the south, they had painted slogans during the other regime: to obey, to fight, to win. Obedience was done, fighting was over, there had been no victory. Agony was left, and a sense of suffocation.

"Oh, shove off," the Englishman said. "It's a bloody party."

"Yes," Antonio said. "It's an army of parties."

The sergeant looked up wearily. Bloody arguments. Nothing but bloody arguments. "Look here," he said, "there's a lot of our chaps lyin' out there dead from El Alamein to Tripoli. And it ain't Jerries' bullets in 'em."

"No," Antonio said. "They are ours."

"Bloody well right yours," the Englishman said.

"And our dead?" Antonio said. "Whose bullets are in them in the desert? Whose wound did I carry from Bardia to Mersa Matruh?"

"Antonio!" Adele said.

"What do you want?" Antonio said. He wheeled quickly. The muscle worked in his dark jaw. "When they talk like that it is impossible for me to be silent!"

"I don't want you to quarrel in my house," his mother said.

He bit down upon his lip. He made a visible effort to restrain himself. At Mersa Matruh the bandage had been black with his own blood. "Va bene," Antonio said. "Excuse me," he said to the Englishman.

"That's all right," the sergeant said. "Just hold your water and let's have a party."

"Yes," Ugo said, "it is the New Year."

"He loses his temper," Adele said.

"Mamma!" Antonio said. He was divided from all of them. There was nothing they understood about humiliation, and this sense of impotency and shame. "Please. It's finished!"

He made again one of those abrupt melodramatic movements of his. There was an uncomfortable silence. "Here," the Englishman said, "let's have another bottle of vino." He called out: "Mimi! Vieni qua!"

"Sì, sì!" Mimi cried. "Vengo!"

Bloody young Eyetie. They were all a bloody lot, the sergeant thought, the young ones, hanging around the cafés, black-marketing, with their hair oil and their swimming hot eyes. Bloodier than Wogs, standing there on the sidewalks, looking at you as though you'd just robbed the poor box. Should have knocked off a few more of them coming up the coast road from El Alamein, the sergeant thought. Better off all around. Bloody beggars. Chap couldn't have a party without one of them hissing at him.

The girl said, suddenly, "But why shouldn't Antonio lose his temper? We are all so careful! So afraid!"

Is she going to pop off too? the sergeant thought.

"There is nothing to be done," Adele said. She was troubled. "Why should one be angry?" she said. "It's necessary to be hard. To be angry is wasteful and stupid."

"If we had men!" Lisa said.

"Men!" Adele snorted. "We have fifty political parties . . . full of men!"

Robert looked at his watch again. "It's almost midnight."

"I'm sorry you are not in New York," Lisa said.

"Stop it," Robert said to her.

"But you would have a wonderful time in New York," the girl said.

"I'm having a wonderful time here," Robert said.

Antonio looked at the girl. At least, there was one ally in the room. She was married to one of his unacknowledged enemies, but she was young, she would know the difference between victory and this kind of defeat. "It is different for you, signora," he said to Lisa, politely. "You will go to America with your husband when the war ends. But us? We will stay here to be punished!"

"Punished?" Robert said.

"Yes, punished," the boy said. "Because we made the war. Because of the regime. But how do you punish us? Tell me, signore . . . how? Do you go and pick the guilty one, and say, he's guilty, him we shoot? This is the bad one, he is responsible, him we imprison? No! The ax on all our necks . . . !" He leaned forward, trembling. His face was flushed and dark. He looked intensely at Robert.

"Don't look at me," Robert said. "I'm not responsible."

"Who is?" Antonio said.

"Christopher Columbus," Robert said. "How the hell do I know?"

But Antonio knew. Yes: in his eyes, the uniform was the same. "When we go into the street," he said, leaning forward, accusing them, because of the uniform, "what do we see? Your colonels, in their big cars, driving with women whose reputations were made in the bedrooms of fascist bureaucrats! With my country's enemies! Or your soldiers, drunk in our gutters. Or your officers, pushing us off our own sidewalks! Oh, the magnificent promises the radio made us! Oh, the paradise we'd have! Wait, wait—there will be bread, peace, freedom when the allies come! But where is this paradise? Where is it, signori—?"

"Antonio!" Adele said.

The boy's head turned fiercely. "I must speak! It's choking me!"

"Go to your room," Adele said.

"The liberatori!" Antonio said. He laughed, a short hard quick laugh. There was no humor in it.

"Go to your room," Adele said.

She took his arm. "Antonio! Do you hear me?" He allowed her to draw him away. "Yes," he said, "I'll spoil the party. The Alleati must have their parties."

"Basta," Adele said. "Enough now."

She drew him out of the room.

Ugo looked at them. "Excuse my son," he said. There was a painful silence. "When the Germans were here," he said, "I hid him—in the cellar. It was because of the arrests, they were arresting all the young who had deserted . . . and sending them north to the factories in Austria, and to the labor camps . . . He was two months in that cellar and I would bring him food." He looked at them, as though possibly they would understand this: the two months in the cellar. "To live with fear, and with hatred, is bad . . . one changes because of it, and yet, when one has only one son, what else can one do? He's so changed . . . Always," he said, "when I went to the cellar, Antonio would ask me: where are the Americans, are they close, why do they stay so long at Anzio? It was difficult for him—a soldier, young, and part of a defeated army—and then, to live like that, for two months, in a cellar . . ."

He did not finish. He means, Robert thought, to emerge into this, to come out of the cellar finally into this.

Outside, in the dark, there was a sudden sound of bells. Of bells, and of guns firing.

They looked up sharply hearing the bells and the guns.

"Midnight," the Englishman said. "Happy New Year's."

"But the guns," the old man said, hearing them. "I hear guns."

"It's the American Army," Robert said, "celebrating."

The Englishman stood up. "Come on," he said. "Let's go out into the garden and see the fireworks. Listen to them."

Pistols, bells, and then the sound of a machine gun.

"It's a bloody mutiny," the sergeant said. "It sounds like a bloody mutiny."

6.

From Porto Bardia to Tripoli. Between Barce and Derna the cliffs dropping to the sea. At El Aden the tanks burning.

The highway, and on one side of the highway, the desert, and on the other the mountains, and behind them, the English.

Is it bad, tenente?

Yes, bad.

Does it hurt much?

There was so much blood, and the blood had turned black, there on the edges of the bandage.

And they were on the truck, lying on the beds and the equipment evacuated from the field hospital, he and Volpini, and Volpini said jump jump when at Bir El Acroma the English had strafed the column, coming over, low, and you could see the flashes, intermittent, in the sunlight, short and fiery, and he jumped, limping grotesquely into the ditch as though the ditch would help. From December fourth to the twenty-third of December. See how he remembered the dates. How the dates clung. How the time was fixed. From December fourth to the twenty-third of December. The Retreat. And then it was Christmas Eve in Tripoli.

Again, again, again. Would it never stop? He had, he thought, firmly clinched himself on the present, denying it, denying those nineteen days, and yet it would not go away. The wound suppurated. The pus was there. The bandage black with blood. The memory did not heal.

No, he thought, lying in the darkness in his room, on the bed, turning his face to the wall, feeling the flush and the heat as though he were in fever, hearing the sounds of the celebrant bells and the guns firing, no, he thought, it was over, it was all part of the defeat, when his world fell to pieces, and nothing, nothing could possibly come of remembering any of it, Bardia or the burning tanks at El Aden, or the planes coming down again in the afternoon with their guns streaking and Volpini saying jump jump there at Bir El Acroma when he had jumped and the plane coming over and Volpini had jumped too late. Jumped, and the truck, in the disorderly column, veering off the highway, had gone over the twitching body there on the cement, Volpini, and he lay in the ditch. That was nothing to remember now for none of it was real except in his memory, and only this was real now: the dark streets, the Americans shooting drunkenly in the holiday night, the lire down, all the whores, and the indigestible bread.

He was Antonio, he thought: the African lieutenant was dead, in the desert, with Volpini, dead with the smoking over-turned tanks and the German motorcyclists racing through the disorderly column, attempting order. What was it Volpini had said of the campaign? The temptation in the desert. But he had meant the empire. The invisible impossible bloody empire. An empire of sand and death and illusion. If Graziani had driven through to Suez it might have been different. If they had mounted the double attack, northern and southern. But the whole campaign, from the first, had been a scandal. It had all been sand and death and illusion and the fiery streaks out of the sky.

Perhaps it had been doomed from the very beginning. Doomed long ago, fixed in some historical destiny, fixed in some ill-fated star of Graziani's, fixed so that the fuel should fail when fuel was needed, fixed so that the shells should lie on the piers in Naples when there were no shells at Mersa Matruh for the guns of the bersaglieri. All of it fixed. Determined far in advance. Reckoned and destined, all of it, before he, Antonio, had been born, or had gone, in his neat-booted ignorance, into the hold of the transport sailing from Augusta.

Now it was over. A campaign. A retreat. A defeat suffered. The truth of all of it, when the documents would be finally revealed, possibly different from what he thought of as the truth. Only the wound, that was to be his truth, the undeniable one, the one documents had nothing to do with, as another's would be his blindness or his handless arm. From Bardia to Tripoli. Between Barce and Derna the cliffs dropping to the sea.

Does it hurt much, tenente?

He could hear the guns and the bells.

And then one had waited so long there in the cellar, and there was always the half-shame that one had deserted, even though the Army was no longer one worth fighting for, and in the battalions the Germans had spread false and misleading rumors, and regiments, full of conflicting stories, had surrendered their arms, and the news of the peace was deliberately kept from the troops. Even though it had been that kind of an army there was the half-shame always because of the desertion. And more difficult because one was young and an officer. Then, lying there, on the blankets, in the cellar, waiting for one's father to come down into the darkness and to feed one. Thinking there in the darkness always about it. Remembering how Volpini had liked to hunt. How they had planned when it was over to have a great deal of hunting and the rabbit stew that Volpini had sworn would taste like no other, and then, the retreat, like rabbits themselves, and the others doing the hunting. Perhaps it would have been better not to have hidden, not to have stayed there, in the cellar, in the darkness, but to have gone north, to have gone into the hills, they were organizing then in the hills, and the combat groups were being formed there. Many had gone off, and it would have been better he knew now, in his room, hearing the guns, to have gone off, to have fought there, in the marshes, in the forests, and even to have died there under those conditions of unequal warfare. For now there was nothing left at all but the corruption, and this house, and the soldiers of those armies he had thought were to be armies that would welcome him, but which did not welcome him, which perhaps despised him as he despised them, coming here to have his mother serve them food and wine, to sit drunken in the dining room.

There was a ripping sound in the night, and he recognized a machine gun.

They could afford to celebrate with ammunition.

In the darkness he got up, moved toward the table, switched on the small lamp, and took out again his bullet. He held it under the light of the lamp, smooth, a little flattened, and he imagined he could still see the slight indentation the forceps made, and still see the Bavarian doctor extending it toward him, held between the clamps of the forceps, saying, "Here, you might want this, a souvenir," on that Christmas Eve in Tripoli.

And afterward he had had such a high fever.

Outside, now, while he turned the bullet carefully and slowly in the lamplight, they were celebrating: the bells all rang, and guns in the hands of those who were involved in his defeat, and now in the continuing humiliation of his country, fired in short happy bursts.

7

I n the bedroom, the sound of bells could still be heard, bronze and heavy. Robert had brought the bottle of cognac with him into the room. The lamp was lit.

She lay on the red bedspread. She had covered herself with the raincoat. She looked quite small and tired.

"Would you like some cognac?" Robert said. "Ugo thinks I was overcharged for it."

"No," Lisa said.

"It'll warm you. Besides, you ought to celebrate the New Year's."

"You celebrate it," the girl said.

"The bartender said it was pre-liberation cognac," Robert said.

"I believe you. It is very good cognac. But I don't want any."

"Okay."

He drank the cognac he had poured for her.

They were still firing their guns, and the bells rang.

He thought of the bell ringer, some priest, cold in the church tower, swinging the great ropes. Now, up there, he assumed, the bell ringer was in the tower, the starlight would be visible beyond the shape of the dark belfry and the hanging swinging bells, and how the sound must be deafening. He would be an old man, like the priests in the church of the Capuchins, the caretakers of the sacred skeletons whose bones they made into altars, and he wore, not sandals probably, but thick army boots, as he had seen some of the priests wear, and a rope was tied around his waist, and his hands would be calloused by the ropes. That priest would make that music, and the soldiers made their own. But the priest wouldn't be drunk. He would be diligently devout. He went toward the bed and sat down beside her.

"It's midnight," he said. "Usually we kiss at midnight on New Year's in America."

He leaned down towards her.

"No," the girl said.

"Why not?"

"I'm tired," Lisa said.

They were all out at parties, he thought, at home; parties at somebody's house or parties at some restaurant, and the shops in Times Square had boarded up all their windows. They were waiting for midnight in his own country, and the crowds were beginning to gather under the electric teletype in the square, moving sluggishly and thickly from the square to the circle, with horns, blowing the horns, pushing, endangering the plate glass, the tin horns blowing and the auto horns blowing, and passing under the marquees of the theaters and in front of the movie houses where, because of the cold, the cashiers in the cages wore their fur coats and the barkers outside the movie houses wore their operatic capes. Then the hats, the liquor, the waiting for the clock to strike; and how, when it did and you were young, you went to the window and blew on a tin horn or rattled a cowbell out into the frosty darkness, and shouted, and when you were older you kissed and shouted. The very last party he could remember having been at on a New Year's Eve he had been very drunk. But here, he wasn't even drunk, there were no paper hats, there were no tin horns, and the girl he had was too tired to kiss him.

"You were out pretty late," Robert said. "Who was the friend? The one who talked so much?"

"A friend."

"Does your friend have a mustache?"

"What?" she said.

"Maybe your friend sings arias through his mustache," Robert said.

"Why should it matter?"

"It doesn't," he said, sitting there. He thought suddenly of something that had happened: they were coming down the Corso, at night, in a weapons carrier, and an MP blew a whistle, and they stopped the weapons carrier, and the MP hoisted a guy up into the truck. He'd been shot. He'd been shot in the foot. It had happened in the dark under the arcade. There had been a girl with the soldier, and then somebody in the darkness of the arcade had shot him. The foot bled into the floor of the weapons carrier. The guy's boot was full of blood.

"No, it doesn't matter," Robert said. "Except you know how the Americans are."

"No," she said. "How are the Americans?"

"Suspicious," he said.

"Really?"

"And jealous."

"What a surprise," she said. "I did not think the Americans were capable of jealousy."

"They're capable. Where were you?"

"It does not matter."

"If you say that again," he said, "I'll—"

"Yes?"

"Break your neck."

"It does not matter," she said.

"Goddamit!"

"Are you angry?" she said.

"No!"

"I thought you were angry," she said. "But I forgot. The Americans are above anger. Only Antonio is stupid enough to get angry."

He took her arms, knowing he was hurting her.

The guns fired sporadically in the distance. They were still celebrating.

"Are you trying to get me to blow my cork?" he said.

"Che dici?"

"Blow my cork," he said. "Steam me up!"

"I?" she said. "Impossible."

"Yes, you!"

"But I'm just a girl," she said. "An Italian girl you met in a war. An adventure. How can I possibly make you angry?"

"Go ahead," he said. "Talk."

"If I annoy you, I'll stop."

"Don't stop," he said. "It'll kill you if you stopped now. Go on. You were being an adventure."

"Well, it will amuse her."

"Amuse who?"

"Some American girl," she said. "Your fiancée. The one you pretend not to have. It will amuse her when you are in bed together. Your story about the Lisa you met in Rome."

"Yes," he said. "She'll love it."

"It will be very funny," she said. "How once in Rome during the war you lived with an Italian girl because she was . . . unlucky."

"Are you finished?" Robert said.

"Yes. I will make a very funny story, no? You see? Why should it matter what I do or where I go?"

"Except it happens to," he said.

"No. It does not matter. It is not important."

He could imagine them firing the guns. They were out in the dark, behind the stadium probably where they held the track events in the summertime, drunk, firing the forty-fives they had picked up or the Berettas they had bought. They might even send up some flares, if somebody had a flare gun.

"It's important all right," he said. "Don't you worry about it being important."

"Yes?"

"Because I like you." Not love you; he noticed that he was careful. She turned away, almost smiling.

"Should I be flattered? Yes. I am flattered."

"I think I will break your neck," he said. He thought of them out in the dark, drunk, and firing their guns. Maybe that was how he, too, should have celebrated New Year's. He had a gun, too. They all had guns.

"You know," she said, "perhaps this winter it will snow, too. Just for the Americans. I think it may now just for them."

She looked hopefully at him.

He took his hands from her shoulders.

"All right," he said. "Tell me what you want. Obviously you want something."

"I? Nothing." She looked faintly astonished. "I have everything, haven't I? You heard Antonio. How lucky I am! I am going to America. They won't escape but I will." She turned away again, painfully. "Che buona fortuna!"

He stood up. She lay there, curled up on the red bedspread, under the raincoat. It was again cold enough in the room for his breath to steam. It was some New Year's.

"Do you like me at all?" he asked.

"Così così . . ."

"Tell me the truth."

"Does it matter?"

"Yes."

Her voice changed. She was not pretending anything now. Her mouth was close to the cold pillow.

"I think I hate you."

He could feel himself drain. Anger, annoyance, desire for her, went away. There was an emptiness, an astonished sort of emptiness. That, and a faintly sick feeling. It was as though he had run into a wall. Or was in a room, suddenly, without doors. That, and hearing the guns, thinking at least out there he would have been drunk and it would at least feel like a kind of celebration.

"But why?" he said. There seemed so little reason for it. There really seemed so little reason for it. "I didn't think I was that bad . . ."

"It was not possible," she said.

Possible? What had possibilities to do with it? He looked into his own emptiness.

"Then why did you start? Why did you tell Nina yes? Why did you have me come here?" Through the darkness, carrying the musette bag, expecting something. Not so long ago.

"Because," she said, "I thought nothing was important any more. Because I thought everybody had a soldier. The Americans were rich, they have so much. I thought why not? Take one too. It's so simple!"

"Wasn't it simple?" he asked.

"No!"

"But it is simple," he said. The emptiness was simple, too. Not feeling at all was simple. Guns and drunkenness were simple. "I was lonely," he said, "you were hungry. What could be simpler? I didn't ask you to love me."

"No," she said. "Just to go to bed with you."

"Yes."

"How simple!"

"Yes," he said stubbornly, because it was so, because it seemed so to him. She did not know how simple that really was. The other things were complex. The being lost, the nights in a long room where somebody shouted in his sleep, or somebody cried, or somebody coughed, that was complex. Thinking was complex. Thinking what a gun was doing in your hand. Why you went on and on when there was no apparent and true reason why you should go on and on. Why at no point you resisted. Why you let it all happen. "I thought it was simple," he said.

"You should have found someone who thought so, too," she said. "You were kind enough, even generous—you brought the food, and I had real coffee, just as we had arranged. And you asked so little . . ."

"I wanted a girl," he said.

"And it was not important how," she said. "Or what she felt. So little—that she should be warm, that she should be here when you wanted her . . ."

"Is that wrong?"

"No," she said. "No. Why should it be wrong if you don't think it's wrong?"

"You needed the food."

"The food! Yes. Didn't I? I did not need anything but the food!"

"I don't care about the other things," he said, slowly. It was a time to be absolutely truthful. "I don't think I care anymore about the other things." He would try. He had never really explained it. The way things had changed. But he would try. Here, in this room, cold enough to make his breath steam. And while a celebration of which he was no part was going on. "I wanted a girl," he said. "I don't think I wanted love. I wanted a girl because I didn't like to have to stand under the trees on the Via Veneto or to go under the bridges. I wanted to get away from the Army. I wanted to have a house I could come to, and a girl there, mine. I wanted it as simple as that, as simple as it could possibly be. And I thought I would just be exchanging something somebody needed for something I needed. Something somebody wanted for something I wanted."

"The black market," she said.

"Yes," he said, "the black market, if you want to call it that. Everything's in the black market now. And I didn't want money for what I had. But you don't want it simple like that, do you? That's wrong. That's ugly. You have to complicate it with love. Oh, you'll climb up in the hayloft all right, but you have to be in love before you climb up the ladder, don't you?"

"Oh," she said, "you are so delicate. You understand a woman so well!"

"I'm a dumb American," Robert said. "You said that before."

"From such a great country! With such sympathy for human unhappiness!"

"We do all right," he said.

"Yes," she said, "and you will make Europe so grateful to you!"

"I'm not interested in Europe."

"What are you interested in?"

"Me."

"Bravo!" she said. "How honest!"

"Yes," he said. "And that's a hell of a lot more than I can say for Europe." He went to the table, now that it was all said, and filled the small glass with cognac, and drank it. The firing had almost died away. Tomorrow, now that it was all said, he could go out with them again, under the bridges, under the trees. He put the glass down. "Well, it was a lovely New Year's." She still lay there, huddled up, not looking at him. He thought of how pretty she had looked the first time he came to the house. He thought regretfully she was still that pretty. Her hair lay blonde and soft on the pillow. "I guess this finishes it," he said. "You figure out some excuse to tell the Pulcinis tomorrow. Tell them my outfit left town. We moved up north." He looked at her. He thought: shall I ask her? No, he thought: she'll say no. "Would it be all right," he said, "if I kissed you Happy New Year's anyway?"

She turned her face deeper into the pillow.

He went and stood beside the bed. "I ought to kiss some-body a Happy New Year's."

He bent down and kissed the visible corner of her mouth. Her face was very cold. He looked at her for a moment and then went out of the room.

8

Once, near Portofino, when she was seventeen, there had been a water snake under the rock near the edge of the shore. Portofino was very white in the sunlight and very beautiful. It was one of the summers she remembered as a very happy summer. It was just before the war. Lying on the bed now, in the silent room, with the raincoat over her, she thought of the water snake curled under the rock. The snake in the water was a dark green, and the water lifted him, and he floated, dark and green and sinuous. On the blue bay two young men were sculling. Their boat looked so fragile. Their naked shoulders glistened. She watched again in the silence their swift and skillful passage across the soundless water. Then she remembered the stick she had taken, and how with the stick she had thrust and poked at the water snake. The rock was possibly his home. The water his true element. And down from the sunlight came her intrusive stick, disturbing the water and the snake, and driving him from his safety, from the place he had chosen there under the rock, and lying there, not being able to cry, remembering Portofino, how white it was, how beautiful, and how long ago, she regretted and almost pitied the snake she had driven out so long ago in that summer she remembered as being one of the few happy ones.

So it was over, she thought; and now? She had gone to the French that first morning, foolishly, thinking the French were different. There was no difference. She lay, covered by the raincoat, and the small dull faintly anguished thoughts went on in her head. She remembered a picture of herself, in a white dress; it was the summer she was engaged, but then she had not really liked the boy. Now, infinitely distant, there was the portrait, the white dress, the eyes of somebody who had been young. Perhaps she would be able to go back to Genoa; perhaps, in the morning, when she awoke, the war would be over, and then she could go back to Genoa, and see Portofino again, and everything would be in the past: a dream one had had during a very bad time, and in that dream she had done certain things, and waking she would forget them.

She thought: we do finally what we thought we were incapable of doing, and it is less than we thought the doing would be, and at the same time more. And nobody listens, nobody cares, one is alone. There are no drums, no overture, no curtain rising. The audience is cold, or asleep. And yet—could she have? Could she have gone on? No, it was impossible to have gone on. It was only possible if there was love. He was right in saying that love would have made everything excusable. But there was no love. He did not want love. He wanted something else, something that had only the appearance of love, and it was better that it had ended, and tomorrow she would leave the house, and that would be the end. She should not have returned that morning when she went to the Frenchman's hotel. It did not matter that there had been no place for her to go; she would have found a place. Nina was wrong: it was not the same for everyone. For everyone it was different. She could not do it. And her thoughts went on: Portofino, the white dress. Roberto sitting drinking vermouth, tomorrow it would be all over, small, faintly anguished, fading into each other.

Antonio stood in the doorway. "Signora," he said. "Yes?"

He hesitated. "Are you ill?" He did not try to come into the room. "It is so cold," Antonio said. She stood up, brushing her hair back with the flat of her hand. He watched her take a comb from her purse.

"I wanted to apologize . . ." he said, hesitatingly. Your husband is an American . . ."

"He was not insulted . . ."

His face darkened. "They are not all bad—but it's hard for me to distinguish. I am always angry. Besides," he said, "our women . . ." He looked contemptuous. "They are worse than the soldiers. The soldiers have some excuse."

She sat in the front of the small dressing table, brushing her hair. Her face turned briefly to look at him. She did not say anything.

"At least," the boy said, "it is possible to respect you. You have not soiled yourself."

The comb paused.

"One should respect one's countrywomen. Not to feel they are degrading one . . . isn't that true, signora?"

"Yes," she said.

"I wanted to tell you this," Antonio said. "Because you are one of the good ones. You make me feel better."

She looked at him. He was holding something in his hand.

"What is that?"

He glanced down. The Bavarian officer's bullet lay in the palm of his hand. The light touched its flattened copper.

"My souvenir," he said. "A British one." And as she looked questioningly at him: "A Bavarian surgeon took it out of me in Tripoli. On Christmas Eve. It's all I have of my war."

He balanced the ugly pellet on his palm, and she watched, fascinated. "We all have our souvenirs," she said, turning back to the mirror, brushing her hair. But he did not go.

"I was wrong," the boy said, standing there in the doorway. "My mother thinks anyone who escapes is lucky—yes. And she's right. Go away, signora—do what they tell you. Go to America . . . at least, there one can stop one's memories. And ask your husband to excuse me."

"There is nothing to excuse," she said.

"As for me, who knows?" Antonio said. He smiled again, unpleasantly, in spite of his apologies. "Perhaps I'll turn thief. Stealing is fashionable, too—and with a gun, well, one is a little more equal. One can—yes, steal tires. That's a soldier's profession now—stealing tires and changing their treads. Perhaps I'll steal tires. Or who knows? Go north . . . rediscover my courage . . . and in the hills die with the look of a patriot." He paused: "Well, buonanotte, signora."

"Buonanotte, Antonio."

"And remember: go to America, signora. In the end, one is happiest far away from the scene of one's mistakes . . . or one's sufferings . . . And Europe is only that: a continent of despair." He went out, with his apologies and his despair and his intenseness, all belted into that raincoat.

In the mirror, she thought that at last the face would either laugh or cry. It must either laugh or cry. It could not stay like this, neither laughing nor crying. He had apologized! He was contrite! He offered her advice! She would laugh. The face must laugh. But she did not laugh nor did she cry. She brushed her hair, carefully, mechanically, over and over, in the mirror.

9.

They came into the dining room, shuddering with the cold. Outside, the bells and the guns had ceased. "Show's over," the English sergeant said. He held Mimi's arm. "It was like a bloody mutiny." They all came into the room. "Bring us another bottle of vino," the Englishman said.

Mimi was pleased.

"Tutti i soldati sono pazzi, non è vero, Signora?" she said to Adele.

"Sì, tutti," Adele said.

Mimi went off for the bottle.

"My gel's almost her age," the Englishman said, looking after her. "Still has her pigtails down, me missus says. Must be the sun and the vino makes the difference."

"Are you alone?" Ugo said to Robert. He was sitting at the table with the bottle of cognac.

"Yes."

"And Lisa?"

"She's tired. She's in the room."

The bell in the hallway rang; then the door was knocked on, loudly.

"Chi è?" Adele called.

There was a noise of voices in the hallway. There was an angry voice among the voices they could hear. Adele went out of the dining room, quickly, follow by her husband.

"Row, sounds like, doesn't it?" the Englishman said, indifferently.

They came into the dining room then, a curious procession: Adele and Ugo together. There was a soldier, too. The soldier limped slightly. The angry voice was his. There were two Italian carabinieri with him. They wore black polished puttees and they carried slung carbines, and small black holsters with berettas. Above the visors of their hats shone the insignia of the police: a golden sunburst. Behind the carabinieri, Mimi came, her face frightened. Robert looked at all of them as they trooped into the dining room.

The soldier who limped said, "That's her! This is the place. She's the one got me sick."

He meant Adele.

"Calmo," one of the carabinieri said. He was the better looking and the more authoritative of the two. He tried to quiet the limping soldier. "It will be taken care of. Which is the one you said telephoned?"

"Her," the soldier said. "The old bitch."

"Here now," the Englishman said, standing by the table. "Take it easy with the names."

"Signora?" the carabiniere said.

"What does the drunkard want?" Adele said.

She did not look at the soldier who limped. She looked at the handsomer and the more authoritative policeman. Her eyes had a hard sharp blackness. She had crossed her arms across her breast, and a cigarette smoked between her fingers.

"Did you solicit for this American," the carabiniere said, "a woman named—" He consulted a small black notebook. "Maria Galluzo, who lives on the Viale Angelico 38?"

"I solicit for no one," Adele said.

"What is it?" Robert said. "What's the matter?"

"Niente," Adele said. "Do not concern yourself."

"That's a goddam lie," the soldier who limped said. "She telephoned. She called that tart up."

"Did you telephone, signora?" the carabiniere asked, politely. He obviously did not care too much for the limping soldier.

"Yes, I telephoned," Adele said. "The drunkard whined to me how lonesome he was."

"He asked her all right," the Englishman said. "I heard him ask the old lady."

"Now," Adele said, "the drunkard comes to my house with accusations."

"She was sick!" the soldier said.

"So?" Adele said. Now she looked at him, but with enormous contempt. "It was probably another American who made her sick."

"Did you know, signora, for what purpose you were telephoning?" the carabiniere asked. He was still polite. He held the small black notebook in his hand. The edge of his carbine stuck up beyond his shoulder.

"I know nothing," Adele said. "I telephoned. What the girl does later is her own business."

"And of the police, signora."

"Then go to Maria Galluzo! My house is a good house."

"One must look for the source of the infection," the carabiniere said, smoothly and patiently.

"She was in on it," the soldier said, loudly and angrily. "They're all in on it."

"Calmo, amico," the carabiniere said.

"But she made me get sick!" the soldier said.

"What did you expect her to make you?" the Englishman said. "A bloody hero?"

"Then it was simply to introduce him, signora?" the carabiniere said. "You did not know the profession of this Maria?"

"She's a girl without work," Adele said.

"Sì, of course," the carabiniere said. "They are all girls without work. Exactly, signora, what kind of a house do you have here?"

"A house," Adele said.

"And the soldiers?"

"I serve wine and eggs. Is that a crime?"

"One has not yet said there is a crime." He turned, very elegant and tight and black in his uniform. "And this one here, the little one?" He indicated Mimi.

"She is my maid."

"She lives here?"

"No. She lives with her family."

"Sì, sì," Mimi said. "With my family. We live in the Trionfale."

"Show me the house, signora," the carabiniere said. "There are other rooms, I suppose."

They went out of the dining room. Adele went first. There was a look of resignation and distaste upon Ugo's face. Robert noticed that the old man still carried a newspaper under his arm.

Adele knocked on the bedroom door. Lisa opened it. Her hair was combed, and the lamp was lit on the table beside the bed. The lamplight seemed to emphasize the color of the bedspread.

"Ah," the carabiniere said. "Buona sera. Do you live here, signorina?"

Robert could see her look slowly at all of them gathered in the hallway. He realized there were many of them.

"The signora is the wife of this American," Adele said.

"So?" the carabiniere said. "Congratulations. Your identity card, please."

Lisa waited. She seemed to wait for something else to be said. When they did not say it, she went to the table and took up her purse. She drew a small square card from her purse and brought it to the door and gave it to the carabiniere.

"Grazie," the polite carabiniere said.

He examined the card.

"You are then this American's wife?" he said. He smiled at Robert.

"Yes," Lisa said.

"You have the documents, of course."

"The documents?" Lisa said.

"Of the marriage. One usually has such documents." He smiled at both of them, at Lisa and at Robert. His smile seemed to acknowledge the ease of having those kind of documents.

"No," Robert said. He came closer to the bedroom and went in and stood beside the girl. "I have them. But not here. I have them at my billet."

"So? How unfortunate." The carabiniere took out another book with a longish black cover. He began to write in the book. The slip of paper on which he wrote had straight heavy black lines.

"Tomorrow," he said, "you can show them to the magistrate."

"What magistrate?" Robert said.

"At the questura. The signora knows the address, I think."

"Yes," Adele said, "I know it."

"So I thought." He finished writing. He tore the slip out of the book of slips. "At eight o'clock in the morning," he said.

He held the slip out toward Lisa.

"Wait a minute," Robert said. "Why should she have to go to the questura? I told you we were married!"

"Do I question it, signore?" the polite carabiniere said. "But there has been a denouncement against this house. Unfortunately, the signora does not have her marriage documents, and she lives here."

"We have a room," Robert said.

"Of course: a room. Rome is full today of just such rooms." He extended the slip politely. Robert watched Lisa take it, blindly and automatically. He watched her stare at it.

"Tomorrow, signora. At eight o'clock. May I suggest you search well for the documents? The magistrate is difficult."

He touched his cap with the insignia of the sunburst on it. "Buona sera."

She was staring unbelievingly at the white slip in her hand.

"Andiamo," the carabiniere said to the less handsome and the less authoritative one. They began to move quietly toward the door.

"Ain't you going to do anything about the old bitch?" the limping soldier said.

He stopped the carabiniere.

"When the nature of the house is proved, amico," the handsome one said.

"Shove off," the Englishman said. "You've done enough."

They went down the hallway together. Their guns stuck up above their shoulders. Their uniforms were trim and black. The door slammed.

She was still staring at the slip of paper in her hand.

10

So that, unforeseen, because it was not possible to foresee this, or anything like this, not having thought when he came across the Ponte Milvio that anything except the simple thing, the bare exchange, would happen, Robert heard the carabinieri go, the closing of the door, and then the door opening again. And Antonio, glancing backward, came into the house. The boy came toward the bedroom.

"Mamma," he said to Adele, "what did the police want here?" He was frowning. He must be cold in that raincoàt, Robert thought: the two of them wearing raincoats, they must both be cold in them. But he must sleep in it. He sleeps in the raincoat and he stands in front of the mirror combing his hair to a point on the nape of his neck. "Mamma," Antonio said again, when Adele did not answer him, "what did the police want here?"

Or anywhere, Robert thought; what did they want anywhere? Around the stone bases of the bridges sometimes, leaning over, you saw the water swirling, caught there, a furious wrinkling, and what was caught in the water, in the passage of the water down to wherever the Tiber emptied, swirled with it, helplessly: broken branches, the discarded souvenirs of love, fruit rinds, whirling there, involved in the life of the river. And it was deep, he remembered: though it was a narrow river, it was deceptively deep. The Englishman shuffled uncomfortably. "Well, I better shove off." He wants to get out, Robert thought: it's gotten too deep for him too. He's swirling in it. "Come on, Mimi: show us the door."

"Sì, sergente," the little girl said.

"Bloody party it turned out."

They went away. And I can't, he thought: not now. Though why? What keeps me? What's there to really keep me if I went out the way he went, just out of the door, back across the bridge: that's the way I came, that's the way I can go.

"Che disgrazia," Ugo said. "To come into one's house . . ."

And she was staring at the slip of paper. There could not possibly have been that much written on it: a name, an address, an hour, a charge. And yet she stared; at that official handwriting, at the penmanship of strangers. Don't, he thought: don't; there's nothing there, you've read all there's there to read; and watched her. They don't understand yet, he thought; they don't know how the water's swirling, carrying us all downstream, and how deep, how cold it must be this time of year, with no sun, the grass withered on the banks, the dead leaves and the broken branches and the dirty rinds of fruit all flowing and being dragged downward. And then she said:

"I'm not going."

With something in her voice that must have puzzled them, but which they only interpreted as a feeling possibly of shame, of disgrace, of misfortune, and thinking of it like that, all that was necessary they thought was to comfort her, to solace her, to reduce whatever fear she might have.

"But my dear," Adele said, "one must," and, of course in her world one had to, a slip of paper from the police being an inexorable summons. He was to remember, later, that moment: how she stood there, with the slip of paper in her hand, and the variety of expressions on the faces of the others; and he had a bad sense of what his own expression must be. Because of the other knowledge which, standing there, he did not permit himself as yet to think of, and which, of course, was determining all the things she must have felt, perhaps even knew now, with a prophetic certainty, from the moment the carabinieri came into the house and knocked on her bedroom door, and stood, in their polished boots, politely asking their questions.

"But, Mamma," Antonio said, looking at all of them, "what is it? I don't understand."

So that, finally, he said, with difficulty, trying to control the expression he knew his face must be wearing, "Why must she go?" Adele shrugged.

"It is the police."

As though that explained everything, the inevitability, the resignation, the point beyond which it was useless to protest.

"To hell with the police," Robert said.

And the woman, with that knowledge of something he did not yet possess, the knowledge perhaps that had sharpened and brought to that gleam the hard blackness in her old eyes, and set that dry old bitter mouth, said: "But then, they will come here for her."

"Mamma," Antonio said, desperately, "I don't understand!"

"No," Lisa said, again. "I will not go!"

He and Antonio, he thought; neither of them understood. But Adele did; it was all in that previous knowledge. "My dear," Adele said, patiently, "it is worse not to go." And he pushed forward, reluctantly, toward that knowledge of hers. "What can they do," Robert asked, slowly, "if she doesn't go?"

"To you?" Adele said. "Nothing."

She stands there, Robert thought, like a collection of bad knowledge. Her hair is that dirty gray, she can't sleep at night, she lies there in that bedroom coughing and smoking and sleepless, and the old man reads his newspapers. I never did understand entirely what went on in this house. "You are a soldier," Adele said. "The soldier is always innocent. But the girl—"

"What happens to the girl?" he asked.

I am waiting for her to tell me, he thought. This is New Year's Eve. They shot their guns off to celebrate it. The mother has dirty gray hair and the old man dribbles cigarette ash on the crotch of his pants and the son combs his hair like that. How do I know who these people are? How do I know what she is? How do I know I'm not being taken?

"What happens to the girl?" he repeated.

He watched Adele. She was the source of knowledge now. She would tighten this vise that enclosed them all. He did not look at Lisa. He was aware of the movement of her hands. How they were twisting, slowly.

"If she does not report to the magistrate," Adele said, "they will come here and arrest her anyway and take away her identity card . . ."

"So what?" Robert said. "Let them take it away."

"You are an American," Adele said, "you do not understand. In Europe, without an identity card, one doesn't exist . . ."

If she would only stop twisting her hands like that.

"But, my dear," Ugo said, "there is nothing to worry about."

"No," Adele said, reassuringly.

"Tomorrow you both go to the questura," Ugo said. "And in the court you will simply show the magistrate the marriage documents. They will dismiss it. A mistake . . ."

"But I've done nothing," Lisa said, appealing to them.

"Of course, my dear," Ugo said. "It's a formality."

"They always make trouble for the innocent and not for the guilty," Adele said.

"Mamma," Antonio said.

"It's nothing," Adele said. "You must not look so worried. Mistakes happen. Ugo, go make a cup of coffee."

The old man patted Lisa's arm. He was distressed by the look on the girl's face. So many things happened nowadays. "Control yourself, cara. It's really nothing."

He went toward the kitchen to prepare the coffee.

Robert heard them. The voices, consoling or explanatory. Perhaps he was wrong. Perhaps they were, as they seemed, good people. Perhaps she was what she really seemed. One came, through cold streets, seeking a certain warmth. But the simplest things became difficult. He could not look at her face. She will blame me, he thought. She will think I am responsible. Am I?

"Adele," he said, slowly.

"Yes?"

"What if we aren't married? I mean, what if I can't find the certificate? If I can't prove our marriage?"

There was a perceptible pause and an almost visible change in the woman's face.

"That would be bad," she said.

"Bad?"

"For Lisa . . ."

"Exactly how bad?" he asked.

"Tomorrow morning she would go to the questura," Adele said. He listened intently. He watched her thin and old and perhaps unkind mouth. The knowledge was coming to him now. "There she would be questioned. If she cannot prove she is married, or that she works, then she is taken away from the questura in a police truck . . ."

"Where?" Robert said.

"To the hospital for the doctors to examine."

"Examine?" he said.

"To see if she is sick. And if she is sick, then one goes to San Gallicano."

"What's San Gallicano?"

"A terrible place, Roberto."

"And then?"

"If it is the first time, she is given a small sentence. And cured. And then, later, when she is released, she is given a card. The small yellow card . . ."

Lisa whimpered. It was a little, terrified, and sickening sound.

"One gets a card of the professional," Adele said, looking hard and directly at him. "It is stamped. Officially. And one reports every week. One has to carry it, always. Wherever one goes."

"But what if she's not sick?" he said, driving himself toward all the knowledge. "What if she's innocent?"

"When the doctors examine them, there are no innocent girls. Sick or healthy, innocent or guilty they are all given a yellow card. You see? It would be very bad, Roberto, if you and Lisa were not married."

So that he had it all now, all the knowledge necessary, everything that was inevitable for him to know, and the vise was completely tight. In the kitchen the coffee had boiled. He saw Ugo come out of the kitchen, carrying four cups and saucers on a tray. He saw the steam ascend from the coffee cups.

"Adele," he said, painfully.

"Yes?"

"There aren't any marriage documents."

Antonio leaned forward. His face was all profile.

"What did he say?" he said to his mother. He was almost hissing. "Mamma, what did he say?"

"None?" Adele asked, not quite believing him.

"None," Robert said.

"Mamma, what did he say?" Antonio said again.

"They are not married?"

"No," Adele said, "they are not married."

The boy turned quickly. His face thrust at Lisa. "It's true, signora? Is this true?"

Lisa shrank away.

"Let her be, Antonio," Adele said. Ugo stood, holding the tray of steaming coffee.

"Another one!" Antonio cried. "And this one I thought was good! This one I apologized to! This one I praised!"

"Shut up," Robert said.

"Are none of them honest?" Antonio cried. "None to be trusted?"

"Antonio, she suffers!" Adele said.

"I suffer too!" Antonio cried. "Whores and thieves!"

"Adele," Robert said, thickly. "Get him out of here."

"O patria mia!" Antonio cried. "How they dishonor you!" He turned viciously to Lisa. "Did he pay well, the American? Tomorrow you'll see how well they pay!"

"Antonio!" Adele said.

Robert grabbed him. "Get him out of here, Adele, or I'll knock his teeth out!"

Antonio pulled himself free. "Whores and thieves!" he cried. He spit on the floor. Narrow-shouldered, belted into that eternal raincoat, he turned and went down the hallway and out of the house, slamming the door.

Stupidly, his face full of pain and unhappiness, the old man stood with his tray of coffee cups.

"And you," Adele said to Ugo, "what are you standing there with the coffee for?"

Shaking his head, the old man carried the tray into the bedroom and set it on the table.

Robert stood there. He could feel the sickness inside him. "Adele, what am I going to do?" he said.

"You? She's the one will suffer, not you."

Lisa moaned. She sat on the edge of the bed.

"Ah, poveretta," Ugo said.

Robert went and knelt down beside her. He put his arm around her shoulders. The sickness was there inside him. The sickness, and something else. A feeling something had finally happened he had not foreseen, and could not have foreseen. Am I responsible? he thought. He had only come through the darkness seeking warmth. He had not wanted to sleep any longer in a room full of soldiers. He had wanted a girl.

She was shaking with a deeper cold than the coldness of the room. He could feel the shaking of her body.

"I'll go to the questura with you," he said to her. He pushed the hair back from her face. "I'll go to the questura too. You're my girl. A guy can have a girl in this goddam country, can't he? Adele, I can tell them she's my girl, can't I?"

"Of course."

"They can't hold her if she's my girl," he said. "They can't send her to San Gallicano or whatever the name of it is if she's my girl."

Adele did not answer.

"Can they?" he said.

"They are afraid of the disease in the city," Adele said.

"In the Piazza Colonna last week they arrested a hundred girls on the street," Ugo said.

He heard her voice then. It was small, muffled, painful.

"Adele," she said.

"Yes, dear?"

"Why does he hold me, Adele?" she said to the dark tall woman. "Why does he hold me?"

"Roberto wants to help you," Adele said.

Her lips were dry and the shaking did not stop.

"He is only holding me for San Gallicano," she said, sitting there on the edge of the bed, and her body shaking. Her hair fell forward, masking her face.

"He shouldn't hold me," she said.

"But there is no place to go, my dear," Adele said.

"There is always a place to go," Lisa said. "Please, Adele. Tell him not to hold me."

"No," Robert said.

She struggled. Sitting on the bed, with her hair fallen forward, she struggled. "I said no," Robert said. Struggling then, she began to cry. The sound of her crying was painful, too. It was a hopeless kind of crying. He watched her tears. He could feel the illness inside himself. What can I do? he thought. What am I responsible for?

"Idiot!" Adele said. She went to the table. She tasted the

coffee. The coffee was cold. Ugo's face was full of an old man's sympathy and misery. "Go warm the coffee," Adele said.

Ugo picked up the tray again. His head shook. "Che mondo," he said, going out of the bedroom.

Adele came forward and stood in front of the bed. There was a look of vexation on her face. Robert noticed how at the corners of her mouth the hair grew, dark and shadowy. "Madonna mia!" Adele said. "What is the disgrace? You crawled into bed together. That should be the least of your sins!"

Clumsily, Robert stroked her arm.

"Lisa," he said.

"What fools," Adele said, "what fools I'm lost among! To throw oneself into the river because of the police! If I had gone to the river each time they knocked, I'd be dead and drowned a hundred times! Where is the other fool with the coffee? And you," she said to Robert. "Now you've got her into trouble, take her in your arms. She's frightened . . . she wants to be Tosca! Take her in your arms!"

Clumsily, he put his arms about her.

"Listen to me," Adele said. "Tomorrow Lisa will go to the questura."

"No," the girl moaned.

"Yes," Adele said. "Then we'll see. What can they do? You crawled into bed together. Ugo," she called, "must I do everything myself? Come with the coffee!

"Is she still crying?" Adele said. "Well, let her cry. Tomorrow we'll have a festa. When she comes home, free, and it's all nothing, we'll have a festa. Madonna, they bomb each other, they destroy cities—but a girl in bed is a crime. Here, go away. Let me sit with her."

She pushed Robert away.

"She had to take an American!" Adele said. "With one of her own this would not have happened."

The next day there was hardly any sun, and in another country with another climate it would have snowed. The sky looked like snow, but no snow fell. The day was raw and interminable.

All the celebrations were over. Behind the billets there were accumulated piles of beer cans and emptied bottles of cognac. It was a new year and the same war. But it was a war far away from this city. The things that happened in the city now were part of the war, of course, no matter how far away the war got. In the failing gray light of the day the gardens looked shabbier than ever. The city had no beauty now. The river had no history. When you stood on one of the bridges and looked at the city, you thought of home, and were depressed, and it seemed, because of the grayness over everything, that this war had been going on forever, and it would never end. In the newspapers there was the continuing crisis of power, and the usual number of suicides and murders, and the schedules of the opera, and a notice of the dedication ceremonies recently performed at a military cemetery. The number of raids upon the bad houses, and the houses of suspected fascists, and the houses of the counterfeiters of occupation money, seemed to have increased. There were divisions fighting in the mountains. Their troops came into town wearing thick sheepskin parkas with lined hoods. At night the officers' clubs were crowded. At the government buildings the traffic was heavy and the official papers, of all descriptions, and countersigned by a major or a lieutenant colonel, lay in their wire baskets and were eventually transferred to other wire baskets. One lived peculiarly, and only at odd moments did the actual peculiarity of one's own life become altogether clear.

Now Robert was lying on the blanket on his cot in the long room in which his company was billeted. The room was in the basement of what had once been a fascist officers training quarters and the closets the soldiers now used had formerly been used by the junior officers of the black shirts and their articles of clothing were all neatly listed on a slip of paper pasted inside the closet door. The company's cots were evenly distributed down the length of the room, eighteen beds precisely made and precisely blanketed, and a precise three feet apart, with the heads and the feet of the beds alternately turned toward the wall or toward the center aisle, and in front of each bed there was a foot locker, some of wood and some made of old ammunition boxes, and under each bed there was a depressing arrangement of military boots lined up toe to toe, all of them polished, and all their laces knotted.

On the cots, in fatigues, the soldiers were asleep, with their legs awkwardly apart, and that day's issue of the military newspaper over their faces, so that only their concealed heads under the newsprint had any actual privacy. Down at one end of the long room, at the moment, the end nearest the door, there was a crap game of about the usual intensity going on, and they were using a foot locker as a backboard for the dice. Now and then the door would open and a soldier, washed, coming from the shower, would enter the room, carrying a khaki towel, and a soap dish, and a comb, looking very scrubbed, and every time somebody entered the room the door would slam, loudly, and the sleepers would stir restlessly under the newspapers, and then somebody would say close the goddam door, and kick it, and the door would close again, loudly, and then somebody else would come into the room, slamming the door too, loudly, and all this time, undiminished, the crap game went on.

Lying on his cot, the head of which faced the center aisle, and staring at the rather blank door of the closet which had formerly belonged to a fascist officer, and in which the officer had also had, probably, those inspections on a Saturday morning which made all armies only more sinister versions of a boys' school, Robert went back carefully over all of it. He tried to begin again, as he had done before, with the night he had walked over the bridge, in the cold and the darkness, toward the Via Flaminia. That had seemed like the logical point at which to begin. Now he found, lying there, he could not really begin at that point and the point of his actual beginning moved backward in time. Perhaps it had begun with that gray morning when they had come through the straits of Gibraltar, and the deck had been wet with fog, and down in the hold of the reconverted freighter someone had begun to shout, destroying the last fragments of uneasy sleep, that there was land now, where they had seen for twenty-eight days only water and sky, and he had run up on deck, and there it was: Gibraltar, visible off the port side, like a great tooth coming out of the sea, and the airstrip on the island could be seen, and some low massive sheds that must have been hangars. They leaned then over the rail, in the wetness of the fog, looking at Gibraltar, gray and old and toothlike, and then the infantryman, in his slicker, spitting into the sea, said: "Goddam, it looks better on a Prudential insurance policy." And then, in the night again, off Toulon, after all the talk about the spies hiding on the Spanish hills, spies he imagined with binoculars and telescopes hidden up there like planted and fixed and sinister landmarks, there had been the air raids, and it was the very first of the experiences for almost all of them on the ship and probably on the other ships, and the very first experience remained longest with you, the very first time you felt afraid, and the very first time you heard somebody's teeth going in the darkness, and the very first time that that obscene and compulsory praying began, and the very first time you heard how it was somebody else's ship that had been hit as later it would be somebody else's jeep or somebody else's tank or somebody else's squad, and it was not you. Then, enormous and still intact, the convoy had passed beyond the range of Toulon, and a submarine came up out of the depths of the Mediterranean, and then there had been Augusta, and after Augusta, the straits of Messina, and the land very close now, and very green and old and beautiful, terraced up its quietly sloping hills, with villas on the hills, white and pleasant villas, and after the villas, Naples: her dock all blown apart, and the official buildings and the apartment houses and the hotels knocked full of gigantic holes, and all the glass gone from all the windows, and the queerness of a balcony still hanging mutely to a section of ruined wall, and the queerness of a bedroom all exposed to the air with the fancy wallpaper still papering the wall, and the queerness of a ceiling which still remained and from which still hung the saddest of chandeliers. So that the very first time was the most overpowering because it was all new, and the changes began then, the changes in yourself without your even being aware of the changing as it began, descending the gangplank and lining up by squads on the dock, and marching then, in bulky overcoats, rifles slung, looking at the unfamiliar storefronts and the typhoid signs, and hearing the M.P.s holler at the kids begging cigarettes and selling chestnuts on the Via Roma, and seeing the different troops, Moroccan and Indian and Polish and British, all for the first time, on the narrow sidewalks of the very wounded city. Marching, in formation, under the iron helmets, toward the railroad depot and the freight cars, marked in German and French and in Italian, and then, dumping gun and helmet and pack on the floor of the boxcar, watching the landscape go by as the boxcar rolled, not know-

ing what destination lay ahead, how close the war was, seeing
through the slid-back freight car door the foreign countryside:
trees in blossom which were peach trees, and the stone small
very old-looking houses, and a garden or a back yard with a
scraggy hen pecking in the dirt, and then the ammo dumps,
laid out, planned like parks, acres of bombs or shells, long per-
spectives of oil drums and crated rations, and the point at
which it had all begun had probably been there, without his
knowing it, a point that led slowly and inexorably to the night
going across the bridge toward the Via Flaminia. Because hope
and possibility and illusion had begun even then to vanish, and
more and more he had let the idea of his own extinction
become part of the way he lived, and part of the way he felt,
and all the values he put on everything were part of the knowledge and the certainty that he would occupy such a grave as he
had passed himself so many times since: earth no higher than
the surrounding earth, and the crossed sticks planted in the
earth, and a helmet on the crossed sticks, and under the helmet
the dog tags hanging, and the rain falling on all of it. Yet he had
survived, as they all had here in this room, and they were probably the lucky ones, asleep under their newspapers, or coming
wet and shining from the big shower, or shooting dice there on
the stone floor, and they had all, probably, at one time or
another lived with the fact of their own extinction, and it had
changed them, and the point of the beginning of the change,
he thought, lying on the cot, must have been that.

He got up off the cot and went to his locker and took out his
soap dish and a towel and a comb. Down at the other end of
the room, kneeling, Woods had the dice, and he was trying to
get the dice hot.

"Eight," Woods said, "and I shoot twenty."

"I got five says he can't," Cuccinelli said, standing, with one
foot on the lid of the foot locker. "I got five. Who says he can?"

"Eight," Woods said, "and I shoot twenty."

"Five says he can't," Cuccinelli said. "Who's with him? Who thinks he can? Five says he can't hit eight. Who's with him?"

Robert went down the length of the room, carrying his towel and soap dish and comb, and out of the door and into the corridor and there was somebody telephoning in the orderly room and Captain White was sitting behind the first sergeant's desk reading a copy of *Time*. In the big kitchen they were feeding the Italian laborers. The laborers stood on line, holding their tin plates, and a grinning boy, an Italian too, in a summer-issue cap, ladled soup out of an enormous boiler into the tin plates. Two slices of bread, very carefully sliced bread, accompanied the soup. Upstairs, in the rear of the building, below the officers' mess and from which you could see the officers' billiard room, they were searching those Italians who were not entitled to the soup and the two slices of very carefully cut bread and who were about to depart after the day's work. The Italians stood, one behind the other, waiting to be searched, with small apologetic and placating smiles on their faces and their arms slightly raised, and a corporal went over them, from their armpits to their thighs, including the women. He imagined that, later, when the Italians remembered the sort of smiles they had worn waiting on that line they must have experienced the kind of a feeling about the corporal that he would not like to have people feel about him. He went on down the corridor to the shower room.

It was a big room, full of pipes, nakedness and steam. A squat middle-aged man, wearing ski shoes, took care of the water pressure and swamped out the showers afterward. Robert said "Buon giorno" to him.

"Buon giorno, sergente," the attendant in the ski boots said, because they were all sergeants to him. "How's the acqua today?"

"Hot."

"It looks hot all right."

He undressed at a bench, hanging his pants over the back of the bench, and the odors of steam and sweat were everywhere. Under the iron nozzles, the men stood, soaping themselves, and naked there was a difference about the way they looked, as though the military thing went away completely with the uniform, and naked they all looked somewhat pathetic and very vulnerable, even though they sang because of the heat and the steam and the hissing water. He stood, soaping himself too, under the shower, listening.

"Hey, now!" the soldier shouted. He was doing a very active sort of dance on the drainboards. "Hey, now! Ain't this a bitch? Ain't this something?"

"Hey, now!" the soldier said. "Hey, Mac!"

"Yeah?"

"You have an accident?"

"An accident?"

"Something's hanging out, boy. Hey, now!"

The water hissed and poured, and the shower room echoed, and later, dry again, dressed, he went back down the corridor, his hair damp and combed against his scalp. They were clearing the long wooden tables in the big kitchen where the laborers ate, and the tin plates were stacked high, and only the cups of salt and pepper remained looking very abandoned on the long wooden tables. He hesitated in front of the orderly room, because he was not sure of what he was going to do, or the wisdom of doing it; then he knocked and entered the orderly room, and saluted Captain White who was sitting behind the first sergeant's desk still, and still reading the old copy of *Time*.

"If I had a girl picked up by the police, captain," he said to Captain White, standing in front of the first sergeant's desk, "is there any chance of getting her out of it?"

"What police?" Captain White said. "Ours?"

"No," he said. "Carabinieri."

"Who's the girl?" Captain White said. "Dago?"

"Yes."

"What did they pick her up for?"

"For being with me."

Captain White looked at him and flipped over the pages of the old issue of *Time*. "What do you want me to do? Go down to the clink and bail her out?"

"No."

"Who is she?" Captain White said. "What do you know about her?"

"Not much."

"Then stay out of it," Captain White said, "and next time you get laid pick up somebody the police don't want."

"She's not a bum."

"How do you know?" Captain White said. "Stay out of it. Let the civilian police handle it. Those dago cops don't have anything else to do anyway."

"Yes, sir."

He saluted again, and went out of the orderly room, knowing that it was a mistake and that he should not have gone in at all, and then as he went back into the long room he slammed the door loudly, and left it open, and somebody said for Christ's sake close the goddam door and they were still shooting crap. He put his soap dish and his towel and his comb back into the closet and began to dress. While he was putting his shirt on, the door opened again, loudly, and somebody said: "For Christ's sake."

He looked up.

A soldier was standing in the doorway, a big soldier named Jessup, who was a farmer with a small farm up in Vermont, and he had survived an artillery observation outfit, and now he was loaded and he had an owl on his shoulder. The owl was sitting on his shoulder.

"For Christ's sake," somebody said. "Where did you get the owl?"

"In the woods," Jessup said, grinning. He stroked the owl's feathers.

"What are you going to do with a goddam owl?"

"Keep him."

"Keep him? For Christ's sake."

"I'll make him a pet."

"How do you like that. Now we got a goddam owl."

"Hey, Jess, let the goddam owl fly away. I don't want owl shit all over my stuff. Let him fly away."

"Can't," Jessup said.

"Why do you mean, can't?"

"I broke his legs," Jessup said. He went out of the door again, grinning, the owl with the broken legs sitting on his shoulder.

"Come on," the dice player said. "Who shoots?"

Robert dressed, and went out of the room, and when he got out of the building through the same door the Italians had used to depart after they had been searched and out of the gate guarded by the two M.P.s, he began to run.

12

N ow in the late afternoon, Robert waited again in the dining room, feeling the grayness of the day. He was irritable and restless. Ugo Pulcini sat at the table, peeling an apple with a long knife. The old man glanced up at the soldier. The house was quiet and clean. Outside, the late light faded slowly.

"This Papalino," Ugo said, "was extraordinary. Seven languages he spoke . . . and in those days there were always tourists in the city." It was before the war. He peeled the apple and talked. "One day," the old man said, "Papalino was guiding one of your countrymen, a rich American, about the city. And everything he saw, this rich American, he wanted to buy."

At the window, looking out into the withered garden, Robert said, "What time is it, Ugo?"

"Five . . . a little after."

"It gets dark so early," the soldier said.

Ugo continued to peel the apple. "You know in the Piazza del Popolo the great obelisk? Three thousand years old! The Emperor Augustus himself brought it back from Egypt. There it stands, older than memory, and when Papalino's American sees it he insists on buying it. Of course, Papalino is at first reluctant. He is not sure, he says, he can arrange with the government to have it removed. However, for a slight gratuity and a commission, he will contact the proper authorities. This sounds perfectly reasonable to your millionaire. After all, what is it? An obelisk! So he pays Papalino five thousand dollars down, and on the following day he is in the Piazza del Popolo with workmen ready to remove the monument! We laughed in Rome for a whole week . . ."

The light faded. Nothing was visible but the gray fronts of houses, and the cold sky. He said to the old man, "You don't think she'd do anything crazy, do you, Ugo?"

"Who knows?"

"I should have gone with her," Robert said.

"All you could have done was confess she lived with you," Ugo said. "And perhaps the police would have used that as proof. No: alone, there is a possibility."

"What time did you say it was?" Robert asked.

"Five . . . a little after."

"It's dark already," Robert said, staring out of the window.

She had gone off. She had cried in bed. He did not touch her. The last punishment would have been his touching her. He could hear her crying in the dark, separated from him. He lay in the dark, thinking. Nothing would happen. He told him-self nothing would happen to her. If nothing happened to her, then he could go away. It had simply not worked out. It should have been easy but it had not worked out easy at all.

"Roberto," Ugo said.

"Yes?"

"Do you love Lisa?"

He looked out at the fading light. The lamps would be com-ing on now in a city at home. Here no street lamps came on. The encroachment of the darkness was not pleasant.

"It's not a question of love," he said.

"Excuse me," the old man said. He had sliced the apple. He carried the slice on the blade of his knife toward his mouth. "What is it a question of then?"

"She was hungry, I was lonely, that's the story," Robert said.

"Then why are you so concerned?"

"I don't like feeling like a heel," the soldier said.

"Only that?"

"That's the story," Robert said.

The old man chewed the slice of apple. "Listen, Roberto: the clock strikes. But time doesn't end. Only a day."

"So?"

"Yesterday was a crisis," Ugo said. "It turns out tomorrow is also a crisis. What will Lisa do tomorrow?"

The light ebbed. Darkness swept in from the hills. Visibility died. At home, wherever home was, there was light, warmth, ease, one's familiar things.

"That's not my responsibility," Robert said.

"Whose is it?"

"Hers. God's. The world's. How do I know?"

"You see?" the old man said, quietly chewing the apple. "It is a question of love."

He turned away from the window. The small muscles ground in his jaw. "Look, Ugo," he said to the old man at the table. "I'm seven thousand miles away from the Statue of Liberty. This isn't my country: these aren't my people. I went to bed with a girl. She was hungry. All right: the account's square, isn't it? I didn't lie. I didn't say I was in love. I didn't promise her a villa. I played it as straight as I could. Do I owe her anything? Do I owe anybody anything?"

"No," the old man said, gently.

"I've seen soldiers," Robert said. "They'll promise a girl anything to climb into the sack with her. Christ, to listen to them, they're all millionaires back home. They're all going to marry them, put them on a ship, take them back to mamma's electric icebox! And then one bright morning they ship out and there's Maria, weeping into her spaghetti, and no caro Johnnie in sight."

"Yes," Ugo said. "That is true."

"Well, I'm built different, I guess," Robert said. "Why? Ask God. I didn't want to stand under the trees on the Via Veneto.

I didn't want to go down to the banks of the Tiber under the bridges. But I wasn't going to lie. I wanted to make a deal. A simple deal. An exchange. All right, it didn't work out. Perhaps you can't make that kind of a deal, or the kind of a girl you can make it with I wouldn't want anyway. Now Lisa's in trouble. All right, what I can do to help her, I'll do, money or whatever she needs or wants. But Christ almighty don't put the responsibility for what happens to you Italians on my round shoulders!"

"And when Lisa comes?" Ugo asked.

"I said I'll try to help!"

"What a hard people you are," the old man said.

"What a sentimental people you are," Robert said.

"In Italy," the old man said, "we say: when the wife sins, the husband is not innocent."

"I'm not her husband."

"What are you?"

"Il conquistatore!" Robert said. And went out of the room.

Ugo sighed. The knife cut meditatively into the apple. Outside, in the hallway, the doorbell rang. Ugo lifted his head to listen. The voice was familiar. Then Mimi came into the dining room, and behind her, somewhat dusty, her face streaked with tiredness, but apparently as unconquerable as ever, Nina. He looked at her in amazement.

"Look, Signor Ugo!" Mimi cried. "It is Nina!"

Nina swept to the table. She kissed the old man on the top of his thinning hair. "Eh," she said, "where are the flowers? Where's the music? The traveler's home!"

"A quick journey," the old man said.

"Be a darling, Mimi," Nina said. "Put some coffee on. I've a kilometer of dust in me." The little girl smiled and ran out. "So!" Nina said, surveying the room. "Home again. It's good to be back. Up north—what destruction! We're the only city left in Italy, Ugo."

"And Florence?" Ugo asked.

"Cold, and full of soldiers." She shuddered. Antonio came into the dining room. "Antonio!" Nina cried.

The boy stopped. A quick distaste crooked his handsome mouth.

"Where did you come from?" he said.

"Heaven."

"And the beautiful captain?"

"Who knows?" Nina said. "In hell, I hope."

Antonio snorted.

"But what happened?" Ugo asked.

Nina shook her coat from her shoulders. Her hair was again the red that five hundred lire a rinse could make it. "He left me," she said, indifferently.

"Remember, Papa?" Antonio said. "Such magnificent teeth!"

"But how?" Ugo asked. "It was such a great love . . ."

"How does a man leave you?" Nina said, smoothing her dress down at the hip. "He opens a door and he's gone."

The old man shook his head. "Nina, Nina . . ."

"Suddenly," Nina said, "a tremendous confession. He's married. And his conscience bothers him! It did not bother him for four months. His poor wife, waiting faithfully somewhere in . . . who knows? . . . Ohio! At six o'clock in the evening, when I'm in a hot bath, he has to start feeling guilty! And it was such a lovely hotel."

"What did you do?" Ugo asked.

"I threw his toothbrush after him, and slammed the door. Wet as I was! Then I went downstairs and ordered a big dinner."

"On his bill?"

"Of course. And in the dining room, fortunately, there was a British major . . . bellissimo!"

"With magnificent teeth?" Antonio said.

"And a magnificent staff car going back to Rome," Nina said. "So—"

"Here you are," Ugo said.

"Here I am."

"What army comes after the English?" Antonio said.

"You're very funny, carissimo," Nina said.

"How about the Poles?" Antonio said. "They have magnificent teeth, too."

"I prefer you," Nina said.

"Grazie."

"Because you have such a sweet disposition, Antonio mio," Nina said. She turned again to Ugo. "How is Lisa? And Roberto? Come, Ugo: talk to me. I'm dying for news." She went out into the hall. "Mimi, is the coffee ready?" she called.

"What news is there?" Ugo said, following her. "Just bad news . . ."

Antonio stood alone in the room for a moment. In his pocket he touched the cold flattened head of the African bullet. He thought, She is not afraid of me, but she will be, they all will be, some day. The bullet was reassuring. It focused him again. Touching it, he could remember what he was, and what had happened to him, and why he was justified. After a while, he went out of the dining room, too.

The room was quiet.

Imperceptibly, the last touch of daylight ended.

She came in noiselessly, through the door which opened from the garden, with the sky, briefly revealed, dark now, all the light gone. The collar of her raincoat was high up about her face, and she looked, coming into the room in which no lamp had yet been lighted, tired and drained. She came into the room as though she were estranged from this too, the familiar furniture, the familiar walls, and sank tiredly into a chair, huddled into her coat. She was glad the room was empty and dark, and she would have liked the darkness to continue always. She

stared at the room now as though everything in it, during the
time she had been absent from it, had been transformed into
something unfamiliar and even menacing; as though now, even
the simplest of objects, a radio, a chair, a table, had acquired
an ability to threaten her, and to become part of the general
hostility. She sat there, and piece by piece the involuntary
images of her day would rise up into her mind, and she would
look at them in their remembered light like the pieces of some
grotesque and obscene play into whose plot she had fallen, and
then she would, her whole mind shrinking, push them away
again, thrust them back, and then they would return: the
nakedness of the women in the big cold gray empty surgical
room, waiting to be examined; the girl, shrieking, in the truck,
as they drove through the streets, and the girl who spat at
everything; and the hands emerging to touch her, the faces
emerging, professional, official, dry, indifferent, disbelieving.
They would return, and subside, and they left this stony emptiness inside her, this deathlike silence in which she sat.

She was there, in the darkness, when Mimi came into the
dining room, and startled, said, recognizing her, "Oh, signora!
You frightened me . . ."

She heard the little girl come quickly to her. Something
human again, moving, a voice, a distant incomprehensible
desire to be kind, to be sympathetic, when she had gone far
beyond the place where sympathy or kindness could touch her.
"Did it go well?" Kind, the voice, young yet, was kind, gentle.
"Were they bad, the police? I hope it went well . . ."

"Yes," Lisa said, "it went well."

"Povera signora!" Pity; this one was young, this one had
pity. "But you must not worry. I do not worry. I am frightened
all the time," Mimi said, "but it only makes me giggle . . ."

Separate, there was the separateness, and the feeling of
being beyond the reach of their voices, in this stoniness, this
absence of all feeling.

Mimi touched her, hesitantly.

"Would you like a piece of fruit, signora? If you eat something, perhaps you will feel better."

"No, grazie."

"Life is so ugly now," Mimi said, "is it not true, signora?"

"Sì, sì . . ."

"You must not look like that, Signora Lisa." The little girl's hand touched hers. She could feel the fingers endeavoring to express their sympathy. "Is it true you are not married to Signor Roberto? I heard Antonio talking. He was very angry. . ."

She did not answer.

"I don't agree with Antonio," the little girl said. "Antonio talks because he's unhappy. I think it does not matter, the marriage, if one is in love. Do you love Signor Roberto?"

"Please," Lisa said.

"He is simpatico," the little girl said. "For an American he is very simpatico."

There was a sound behind them in the darkness. She thought vaguely: now they will put the lights on. And she did not want the lights on. She wanted this darkness to continue. She wanted it to be always dark. In the darkness, Mimi saw Antonio standing, looking into the room.

"Look, Antonio," Mimi said. "The Signora Lisa is home."

"Yes," Antonio said. "I see she's home."

"The Signora Lisa says everything went well with the police. Isn't that nice?"

She went to the bureau against the wall and turned one of the lamps on. Lisa flinched as the light came on.

"There," the little girl said. "Now we can see each other."

"Go away," Antonio said.

"But I was to fix the dining room . . ."

"Go fix the kitchen," Antonio said. "They're drinking coffee in the kitchen. Go away."

"But I was to fix the room for the evening," Mimi said. She

looked at Antonio. "Va bene," she said, when she saw Antonio's face. She went out of the room.

The images would not go away. She thought if she did not permit herself to feel anything, if she did not think at all, if she did not permit herself to hear, they would go away. The room came back, empty, cold, surgical, and the girls naked in the room. And the hands. They reached out to touch her. All her flesh crawled away with a soundless shriek from that touch.

"Were they pleasant," Antonio said, standing there, "at the questura?"

She looked up dully at him. Yesterday he had come into the bedroom to apologize. He had apologized. Now he stood there, coldly, while the images sank back, disappeared, the hands momentarily went away.

"What?" she said.

"I asked if the police were pleasant. Were they pleasant? They have a great reputation for being pleasant to the women they arrest."

One went up a long corridor. The walls were dirty, and the floor was dirty. The clerks sat, behind their tables. Everywhere there was the unexpressed hostility, the unacknowledged sneer. Now this one, standing, who had been wounded in Libya, and who could not forgive the wound.

"What do you want, Antonio?" she said, forcing the words heavily out of herself.

"I?" he said. "Nothing." They were familiar words; she herself had said once exactly the same words, with almost the same intonation. "I am looking for an honest woman," Antonio said. "Are you an honest woman, signorina?"

She turned her head. The effort to speak was too difficult.

"Go away," she said.

"Shall I marry you?" Antonio said. "Come, tell me: I'm your countryman. I liked you. Perhaps I was even a little in love.

You are very pretty. Shall I marry you now the American has finished with you?"

Dully, she looked at him.

"There are disadvantages, of course," Antonio said. "I can't take you to a hotel like the Excelsior, or drive you to Lake Bracciano in my jeep. Nor do I have cigarettes to sell, nor can I bring genuine coffee for my nice Italian friends. What have I? A wound from a war . . ."

"Antonio," she said, "please . . ."

"I'm stupid," Antonio said. "Of course. What's inside an Italian's head? *La Traviata* and a bowl of spaghetti. Ask them: they know! But now the American has finished with you it's my turn. A slightly damaged bride! But I should be grateful. Even for you, signorina: that after the American, you consent to share your bed with a countryman!"

She tried to rise from the chair. She had to escape.

She could not bear any more.

He came quickly across the room. She felt his hand on her shoulder, forcing her down into the chair again.

"Wait, signorina. Stay a while. I feel eloquent tonight," Antonio said.

"I don't want to hear any more," she said.

"But where will you go, amore mio?" Antonio said. "Come: it's early yet. Business isn't good on the Via Veneto until it's quite dark."

She sank back in the chair. It doesn't matter, she thought. It doesn't matter. Now there was this one. This one was inevitable, too, now, she understood.

He leaned toward her.

"Shall I tell you what I see, signorina, when I look at you?" Antonio said. "Italy's shame. My shame."

"What do you want of me?" she said.

"I?"

"What do you want of me?"

"To be a woman who does not dishonor her country!"

"I haven't dishonored her!"

"Yes," he said, leaning toward her. "And for what? Is it so difficult to be hungry? To be poor? What is it that the Americans give away so generously? A piece of chocolate? A pair of silk stockings? They ride you around in their cars? They can afford it. They have so much chocolate it rots in their warehouses!"

"Antonio!" she said, moving her head away from him. "Antonio, let me be!"

"And now," he said, "the dream comes to its ugly finish. The police! What is one American? There will be dozens. They'll come to you—yes, drunk, stupid, ugly. In some room somewhere. At night. They'll drop their big boots on the floor, sprawl in your arms—the conquerors! And you? Every week to San Gallicano. Every night on the Via Veneto!"

"Antonio!" she said.

"Yes, cara mia: that's what you can look forward to. San Gallicano! That is your paradise. And what shall I say? What shall I feel? I'll see you drinking with them in the cafés. I'll see you walking with them in the park. And I'll suffer. I'll suffer for your dishonor. And I'll spit on the pavement, seeing you, I'll spit!"

"No," he said, putting his hand into her hair. "Don't look down! Don't look away! Look at me!"

Her head writhed in his grip.

"You're hurting me," she said.

"Am I? Not much. Not enough. But one must pay a little: one must suffer a little. Is it just that the decent should have all the hurt, and you nothing? Yesterday in the bedroom I said I respected you. I believed you! You were one of the good ones who did not sell herself to the Americani, I said. I was stupid, no? I am easily deceived. Because I could not tell. One should be able to tell, isn't that true, signorina? You should not be allowed to deceive people. When you walk in the street people should know. They are also hungry, they are also poor, but they haven't sold themselves. People with wounds . . . they ought to be able to say: There's a girl who has dishonored her country. They ought to be able to know immediately! Else how is one to tell?"

He picked up the knife from the bowl of fruit on the table.

"Is it not just, signorina? People should be able to tell."

"Antonio!"

"There is no Antonio," he said. "Who is Antonio? There is only a man with a wound. No, signorina, it's not Antonio who will cut your hair. It is only your country, avenging itself a little . . . and only a little . . . and only enough so that when you walk in the street with a naked head people will be able to tell!"

He held the knife, and in terror and fascination she looked at it, and the knife was between them, and she did not, or could not scream, feeling only the terror drying her throat, and waiting, and it was Mimi, coming suddenly into the room, and seeing Antonio with the knife, who at last screamed.

"Signore! Signora! Aiuto!" she heard Mimi. "Antonio is hurting the Signora Lisa!"

The little girl rushed to hold Antonio's arm.

"No!" she said. "Antonio, no!"

Antonio pushed at the girl. His dark young face was convulsed. One hand lay in Lisa's soft blonde hair, twisting it.

"Sì!" Antonio said.

Robert came almost running into the room then.

"Signor Roberto!" Mimi cried. "Help me!"

There had been first the business with the cigarettes. The passion that had helped to spoil his New Year's. He had been saving it, and he did not know what was happening, except what he could see, Antonio twisting Lisa's hair, the little girl clinging to his arm, the spectacular knife, and besides it was about time somebody in this house was hit. He hit Antonio.

The boy's hand came out of the twisted hair to defend himself, and he fell backward toward the radio. Then Robert stamped on Antonio's hand and picked up the fruit knife. Behind them now, Ugo and Nina, Nina with a piece of bread in her mouth, came into the room.

"Che cosa succede?" Ugo said, frightened.

"With a knife, Signor Ugo!" Mimi cried. "Antonio wanted to cut her hair with a knife!"

"Madonna!" Nina said.

The boy picked himself up from the floor, his face convulsed, the stamped-on hand hanging limply. "Was it not just, signorina?" Antonio said, in agony. "The people should be able to tell . . ." And went out of the room.

"Poveretta!" Nina said, kneeling beside Lisa. "Did he hurt you? Did that animal hurt you?"

"We were talking," Ugo said, bewildered, "in the kitchen . . ."

"It's all right," Robert said. "I didn't hit him too hard. I didn't know what he was going to do with that knife."

"Povera signora," Mimi whispered.

"He needs a keeper, that animal!" Nina said, kneeling beside her, stroking Lisa's hands.

"He's ashamed," Ugo said, suffering for his son.

"Ashamed!" Nina cried. "Some day he'll kill somebody with that shame of his. Go bring a glass of wine, Mimi . . ."

The little girl ran out.

"When will there be peace?" Ugo said, suffering for Antonio, suffering for himself.

"When the animals are in the zoo!" Nina said. She continued to stroke Lisa's hands. She's numb, she thought. She's breathing so quickly. How that animal frightened her!"

"Everything's changed . . . everything," Ugo said, heavily.

The little girl came back into the room, bringing a glass of wine. She gave it to Nina. "Here, cara: drink," Nina said. She held the glass to Lisa's mouth. She's so white, she thought.

She's so exhausted. "I'd have torn his eyes out," she said. "I'd have broken all his bones."

"All right," Robert said.

"What kind of men are you? Stone?" Nina said. "A woman can wait before you help her." She chafed the girl's cold hands. "There, cara: is that better?"

Dully, out of that enormous exhaustion, that darkness, she said: "They would not believe me at the questura."

"Shh, cara: don't talk," Nina said.

"Why should they have believed me?" Lisa said. "It was true. I was what they said I was."

"She doesn't have to talk about it, Nina," Robert said. "Don't let her talk about it."

"Then, afterwards," Lisa said, "they put all of us into a big truck. There were so many girls."

"Non importa, cara," Nina said.

"When we drove through the streets," Lisa said, "everybody looked at us sitting there in the truck. Then some of the girls shouted and some even sang and some spit at the people in the street and some cried. There were so many girls."

"Eh . . . !" Ugo said.

"Were they all bad, Ugo?" Lisa said. "All of them?"

"Eh . . . !" the old man said again.

"Then in the hospital," Lisa said, "they put us into a big room, and they said undress, and when we undressed they examined us. Have you ever seen, Nina, many women together naked in a big cold room?"

"I don't want to see it," Nina said.

"I was so afraid," Lisa said, "of touching anything. I was so afraid of the disease . . ."

She stared so, sitting in that chair.

The old man touched his own forehead, not knowing what one could possibly say.

"Eh . . . but they released you . . ."

"Yes," Lisa said.

"Why should they hold her?" Nina said, indignantly. "She's innocent."

"Yes," Lisa said. "They released me."

"Thank God," Ugo said. And thought: in this darkness, and emptiness, does He exist? Nothing existed: only the darkness and the sound of human suffering. There was a great emptiness, in which all were alone.

She had turned to Robert.

Was she smiling? Ugo had a painful expression of something that was not a smile.

"It will be so much easier now," Lisa said.

"What?" Robert said, not understanding.

"It will be so much easier now that I am what the others are."

"Lisa!" the old man said.

"What others?" Robert said, harshly.

"The women standing on the bridges," Lisa said.

"Now she is being stupid again!" Nina said, with that simple indignation of hers.

"What do you mean?" Robert said. "They let you go, didn't they?"

"For a while . . ."

"But—"

"It was my first time," Lisa said, "and I wasn't sick." Her hands in her lap clenched. "Why didn't you go to the girls on the Via Veneto!" she cried. "Why did you have to come here!"

Ugo again had that overwhelming sense of emptiness: as though they were all lost in a great and hollow space, and there was nothing in that space but the sounds of suffering, and the small gestures of despair.

"No, no . . ." Nina said, caressing her. "It's my fault. Cara, it's my fault . . ."

"Ugo," Robert said, thickly.

"Yes?"

"Take Nina and go out. Please . . ."

"It's my fault, all of it," Nina said.

The gestures—of hope, of comfort, of despair. They were all abandoned in such a space. I'm old, Ugo thought: and I'm tired. We were not made to be happy. Happiness is a condition we have permanently lost. He fumbled in his vest pocket: there was a cigarette there. "Come, Nina . . . let them alone," he said. He took Nina's arm.

I'm sweating, Robert thought. My hands are sweating.

13

Outside, in the wineshops, Robert thought, they are sitting at the small tables with the stone tops. The wine was drawn from the spigots in the barrels. There were no women in the shops. Only the men of the neighborhood playing cards, and the soldiers, drinking. They talked about cards and sometimes about the war. Vermouth was the best and cheapest thing to get drunk on, and it was pleasant. He could have been there, in one of the wineshops, drinking vermouth, listening to the card game.

"Lisa," he said.

He could have been there, pouring vermouth into a tumbler. The wineshop would be small, not too clean, and full of bottles lined up on the shelves.

"If there was anything I could have done," he said, "I would have done it."

"Would you?" the girl said.

"But Adele and Ugo said I shouldn't go to the police. It would be worse if I went to the police, too."

The wine in the tumbler would catch the reflection of the light. There would be only men there, in the shop, and what they would talk about: some particular incident in some particular battle, or the chances of going home and what home would possibly be like, and occasionally a woman known somewhere, in Naples or in Africa, to whom one felt, now, somewhat grateful, and whose memory was pleasant. "I didn't make the war," he said, as though that was the only possible final excuse. "I didn't make the police."

He stopped now, ashamed of having said it. But it did not, he saw, really matter. Nothing he had said penetrated that envelope of numbness she seemed to sit in, or that cold and almost emptied mask.

"There were so many girls," Lisa said. "But where were the soldiers? There must have been soldiers."

"They don't arrest the soldiers," he said.

"Why?" she said. "Shouldn't they arrest the soldiers too?"

"They don't."

"No," she said, "only the girls."

Awkwardly, he came closer to her, and put his hand out, and awkwardly tried to explain, although there was nothing to explain, nothing that could be really explanatory. "Lisa," he said. "Anything you want, ask me. I'll do it."

"Why should you do anything?" she said.

"Because."

"Because of pity?"

"Call it what you want," he said.

He watched then as she drew slowly a card out of her pocket. It must have been kept there all the time. It was yellow and square. The police would have given it to her, very formally.

"And this?" she said. "Can you do anything about this?"

On which her name was written. On which some official had stamped his own designation.

"Put it away," Robert said.

"Why?" she said. "They gave it to me to show."

"Lisa," he said.

"To my customers," she said. "In case there is a doubt."

"Give it to me," Robert said, holding his hand out.

"No."

"Give it to me," he said violently.

"As a souvenir?" she said. "To take home with your German pistol?"

Abruptly, he drew his hand back.

"Oh," she said, "How wonderfully we had it arranged, didn't we, Roberto? How conveniently! You didn't want to stand on the Via Veneto. It was too ugly under the trees . . . and you were too sensitive! It was to be so comfortable for you . . . so accommodating . . . like home!"

"I wanted a girl," he said again, as he said before, stubbornly.

"A girl you didn't love."

"A girl!" he said.

"To bring food to in a little bag. To wait conveniently in bed!"

"Maybe I did," he said.

"And it was so exciting," she said, looking at him, "wasn't it, Roberto? An Italian girl . . . different ways, a different language. Then you could always say—see? I slept with an Italian one, too. Along with the English one, and the Greek one, and the French one!"

"No," he said.

"Don't lie," she said. "Don't lie to me now. It's what you thought. It's what a soldier thinks. And at camp, did you talk about me? Did you compare me? You boasted a little, didn't you? How passionate this one was . . . !"

"But you weren't," he said.

"No: I wasn't, was I?" she said. "I was a disappointment. It was so difficult for me . . ."

"It wasn't easy for me," he said.

"No?"

"No," he said.

"Was it harder," she said, "than it was in Naples? Or in Caserta?"

He did not answer.

"Why should it matter," she said, "what mouth you kiss?

Today a Lisa's . . . tomorrow a Maria's . . . they are all mouths . . . waiting for the soldier." She looked up, with that false brightness, that unnatural flush. "And how generous you are! What is it they pay now, the Americani? Three thousand lire a night?"

"I don't know," he said.

"Three thousand lire!" she said. "Think how much bread that is! How much oil! And for what? A night. One night out of so many. Pay me that, Roberto."

"Will you stop?" he said.

"Why?" she said. "I have the card now. All the technicalities are taken care of. Pay me three thousand lire. It's so much simpler when one pays, and then goes away the next morning."

"You're just talking," he said. "You couldn't do it—"

"Couldn't I?" she said.

"No."

"Then I'll learn," she said. "Antonio says I'll learn."

"Lisa," he said.

"Yes?"

"Tell me what you want." He said it quietly. He stood there, beside her, near the table, controlling himself now, saying to himself he would only say now what was necessary, and no more than was necessary.

"I?" she said.

"Tell me what you want."

"Go home!" she said.

"Christ," he said, "I'd like to!"

"Go home!" she said. "Take your tanks, take your money, take the coffee and the sugar and all your generous gifts and go home!"

"It's seven thousand miles away," he said.

"We don't want you anymore," she said. "The dancing in the streets is over. The celebration's finished. Go home!"

She was trembling. She was standing now, trembling, and he

thought: her too. Antonio, her. Underneath, there's this, the actual thing, how they really feel. And we don't, or don't want to, see it.

He waited.

Then he said, quietly: "Do you remember, Lisa, what you said about the Americans the first time I met you? When I came to the house the first night, and the lights blew out?"

"What did I say?" she said, dully.

"You said they were stupid."

"Yes," she said.

"They were too rich."

"Yes."

"They were liars."

"Yes."

"What did I say?" he asked. "Do you remember what I said? I said we were a little bit of everything. Do you remember?"

"Yes," she said.

"You hate us now," Robert said, standing there. "And maybe you're right. You, Antonio, the kids who throw rocks at our jeeps. Maybe we ought to be hated. I don't know. I'm not much of an American anyway."

He paused. She looked so exhausted.

"It doesn't matter anymore," she said, in that dull and exhausted voice.

"Except it might have been different," he said. "Who knows? Perhaps if I had met you where there was no war . . ."

"We wouldn't have met," she said.

"We might have," he said.

"It wouldn't have been different," she said.

"Why?"

"Oh, Roberto," she said, "it wouldn't . . ."

"Why not?" he said. "All I ever saw of Italy was war." He came closer to her, almost touching her. "But it was different once."

"You wouldn't have come to Italy if not for the war."

She had turned her head away.

"But say I did," he said, urgently, "I always wanted to see Europe."

"You wouldn't have noticed me."

He touched her now. "I always notice blondes," he said. "And I'd have asked the American ambassador to introduce us."

"He would not."

"He would. He'd be that kind of an ambassador. What did you do before the war?"

He never had asked. The bombing in the train at La Spezia he knew, and that she had been hungry, and about the French captain in the hotel on the Corso. Her hair again fell softly across her face, shadowing it. "Did you go to the opera?"

"Please . . ."

"We'd go to the opera," he said. "Which opera do you like best?"

"Oh, Roberto . . ."

"Which opera do you like best?"

"*La Traviata*," she said.

"We'd have gone to *La Traviata*," he said. "Then we'd travel."

"Roberto, please!"

"We'd have seen all of Italy," he said. He urged her into that imagined journey. He drew her closer to him. "Both of us. What town do you like best?"

"Roberto," she said, "stop!"

"Come on: what town do you like best? I'm a stranger here."

"Portofino," she said.

"Portofino? Where is it?"

"In the north. By the sea."

"All right," he said. "We'd go to Portofino. In the north by the sea. Why do you like Portofino?"

Despairingly, she said: "I was happy there once."

"Once?"

"When I was seventeen."

"Would I be happy in Portofino?" he said.

"Roberto!" she said. "Oh, please . . ."

But he held her now firmly, urging her to go with him, to go to Portofino, in the north by the sea, now when it was all dark here, and the city cold, and there was nothing but that great solitariness. "Would I be happy in Portofino?"

"I don't know!" she said, as though she could not bear that journey, or that possibility of happiness.

"I'd be in love," he said. "You're supposed to be happy when you're in love. Would I be happy?"

"Yes!" she said, at last.

"You'd be happy too, wouldn't you? The way you were when you were seventeen?"

"Yes, yes!" she said.

"Then, after Portofino, and after being in love, we'd go to the States, wouldn't we? To America. Just to show them how pretty an Italian girl can be . . ." Close, so that finally a warmth was between them, so that the cold went away, the solitariness, the lostness. "I always take my wives home. You'd go, wouldn't you?"

"Perhaps . . ."

"You'd go, wouldn't you?"

"Oh, Roberto!"

"You'd go."

"Yes, yes . . . I'd go!"

"Besides," he said, "I'd have to show my mother who ate her fruit cake. Tell me what kind of a wife you'd have made. A good one? Would you have made a good wife?"

"Yes."

"How good?"

"Very good."

"All the Italians make good ones, they tell me. But you'd have been one of the best, wouldn't you?"

"Yes . . ."

"Guaranteed?"

"Yes, yes!"

And then it went away: the exultation, the journey of words, the imagined joy. He stroked her hair. "I've brought you nothing but bad luck, haven't I, baby?"

He could not see her face. Against him, he heard her say, brokenly: "Bad, bad luck . . ."

"We turned out to be great liberatori, all right," he said. He reached down now, and took the police card gently out of her hand.

"No, Roberto—give it to me," she said.

"Give you what?"

"The card!"

"What card?" he said, tearing it up. "I don't know of any card."

"Roberto!" she said. "You mustn't do this to me, you mustn't!"

"Do what?"

"This! . . ."

"Why not?" Robert said. He had torn up the card. "Blondie loves Dagwood, doesn't she? Everything happens to them, but she loves him." She was struggling not to listen. "Doesn't Biondie love him?"

He caught her shoulders.

"Doesn't Blondie love him?"

"Roberto!" she said, in a final despair.

"Doesn't she?"

"Yes!"

"Say it."

"She loves him."

"Then kiss him," Robert said. "He just came home from a hard day in the office. Kiss him."

She kissed him at last, crying, she was crying, her mouth against his mouth, hard and despairing, when the door from the garden opened again, admitting the night and the cold, and Adele, her head wrapped in a shawl, carrying a market bag, came into the room, and seeing them, in that fierce and despairing embrace, cried: "Ecco . . ." and Robert took his mouth away from the girl's, and said: "Hello, Adele . . ."

"Dio," the woman said, unwrapping the shawl, "she's still crying?"

"No," Robert said, "she's not crying now. You're not crying now, are you, baby?"

"No," the girl said, crying.

"How did it go at the questura?" Adele asked. She put the market bag down.

"All right," Robert said.

"No trouble? She's free?"

"Yes," Robert said, "she's free."

Adele looked pleased. "What did I say? I said it would go all right. You always imagine things are worse than they are. A little courage, that's all one needs. Where is Ugo?"

"In the kitchen," he said. "Nina's here."

"Nina? Dio, so quickly? But good—we'll make a fine festa. I promised her a festa yesterday . . . wine and macaroni! The Americans like macaroni, no, Roberto?"

"They love it."

"We'll make a festa," Adele said. "But remember: no more tears!"

"No," Robert said. "No more tears."

The old woman picked up the bag. She's good too, Robert thought, in spite of that hatchet face.

"Music," Adele said, going to the hallway, "a little wine, macaroni . . . and no more tears . . ."

She went out.

He put his face against the softness of her hair.

"See, baby?" he said. "Everybody loves you."

"Let me go now," Lisa said.

"All right," Robert said. "First let me look at you."

She closed her eyes and he lifted her face toward him. Tears, exhaustion: and yet the skin still held that fine color, that goldenness. "You're beautiful," he said.

"I'm not beautiful," she said. She tried to free herself.

"Where are you going?" he said.

"To wash . . ."

"Okay: but one kiss first."

"Please," she said.

"One kiss first," Robert said.

He drew her to him again, and kissed her, and then she broke away and ran quickly out of the room.

Alone, he put the radio on. They were playing excerpts from the opera. It was in another language and the room filled with music. He thought: now it'll be all right. Now it'll work. It did not matter so much now that it was cold and dark. He remembered suddenly one of the towns in the south. It was a summer afternoon. Bricklayers were rebuilding a wall of a shelled or bombed house. The war had been in the town only two months before. Now the trowels of the bricklayers made sharp distinct clinks as they knocked the bricks into place and set them in the mortar. They were the old bricks of the house. They were putting up the wall with the same bricks and a fresh mortar. He heard the trowels clinking all the way down the street. Yes, he thought: now it'll work. Now—and then Ugo came in, looking at him questioningly.

"Where is Lisa?"

"Making herself beautiful," he said to Ugo. "And?"

"She's all right," he said. "She's fine now."

They were all fine now. You went on so long and then there was a break, a change, a difference. Things got fine again. He was sure of it. It was cold and dark and all the lights were out but now it would go fine.

"And you, conquistatori?" Ugo said, looking at him. "How do you feel?"

"Me? Great."

"Ah? . . ."

"I'll make them yell Viva la Chicago again," Robert said. "I'll make them hang out flags and throw roses."

Ugo sat down, smiling. The radio was loud. It was one of the big arias from an opera he did not know.

"So," the old man said, "in the end, after the tempest and the tears, everything turns out well. A little love and the world runs smooth . . ."

"How's the macaroni?" Robert said.

"The macaroni's fine. We'll have a real festa. In Italy we say: macaroni and matrimony, if they're not served hot they're no good."

"Italy," Robert said. "Italy!"

"A country blessed by God and cursed by man," Ugo said.

The radio poured out its tremendous music. Robert leaned toward the old man. "Were you ever in Portofino, Ugo?"

"Portofino? Sì. Several times."

"Is it beautiful?"

"Very beautiful. The sea is all blue there, and the town is white. But why, suddenly, Portofino?"

He said it confidentially, leaning toward the old man. "Because I'm going to be seventeen years old in Portofino one of these days."

"You're crazy," Ugo said.

"Sure."

He grinned. But at least now there wasn't that sensation of an enormous and abandoned space in which the small despairing gestures were made and the small despairing cries were heard. Perhaps it was love that peopled that emptiness and contracted all those horrible distances. "Who knows?" the old man said. "Perhaps the war will be over soon. Then you and Lisa can go away to America . . ." He pushed his spectacles higher. "When an Italian girl is in love, Roberto, she can be all fire and cloud . . ."

"Any girl in love is," Robert said.

"But especially ours. You'll see! But take her away . . . Europe's done . . . there will be nothing left soon but the monuments."

"Why don't you get Italy annexed to the United States?" Robert said. "The forty-ninth."

"Suggest it," Ugo said. "I'm willing."

"I'll write my Congressman," Robert said.

"America," Ugo said. "An incredible country. No ruins! It hardly belongs in the twentieth century."

In the hallway the doorbell rang.

Shaking his shapeless raincoat, the pipe in his mouth, the English sergeant came into the dining room.

"Buona sera," the Englishman said.

She'd been happy in Portofino, Robert thought: it was a white town, and the sea was blue. He wanted to see all of Italy: the quiet and undestroyed places, where the sea was blue. There must be many places like that, undestroyed. It was impossible to destroy everything. They never could destroy everything.

"Ah," Ugo said to the sergeant, "you're in time . . ."

It must have been bad in the questura for her. But now it would be different: the difference would be in how he felt. He could borrow the jeep again. They could ride out into the country, or when the summer came swim on the Lido, or visit the old castles. They would clear the mines out of the sea and the swimming would be good. It would be different in the sunlight on the sand and the mines cleared away.

"In time?" the Englishman said. "What for?"

"It's a festa tonight at the Pulcinis," Ugo said.

Yes: music, the opera, the possible swimming when the weather changed, and tonight a festa.

"Do you think we ought to invite England to the festa?" Robert said to the old man.

"Do those islanders like macaroni?" Ugo said.

"Do you like macaroni?" Robert asked the sergeant.

"Hot?" the sergeant said.

"Hot?" Robert said to Ugo.

"Always hot," Ugo said.

"I like," the Englishman said.

"Then we invite him," Ugo said.

"That's right," Robert said. "He is a kind of ally." He liked them all now. They were fine, they were allies, they were finally allies. The macaroni would finally unite them, and there would be a change of heart, a change of feeling. Even Antonio would change too, once he got over Libya. They were good people, they were all friends and all allies, and not everything had been destroyed.

"I say, Yank: wasn't that your gel I saw outside?" Robert turned.

The sergeant's pipe was there, where it had been before, and there was no malice, no threat; it was simply information.

"Outside?" he said.

"In the street," the Englishman said. "She was in an awful hurry. Didn't even have her coat on. Where's the fire? I said. But she didn't seem to hear me."

He could feel the cold and the dark rush back. The opening again of the enormous distances. The wind blowing through the emptiness.

"Where did she go?" Robert said.

"Down the Via Flaminia last time I saw her."

He turned and he began to run. In the hallway Ugo and the Englishman could hear Adele's voice calling, "Roberto! Where are you running? The macaroni is almost ready!" They could hear, too, the violent opening of the door.

Puzzled, the Englishman turned to Ugo. "What's wrong with him?" he said. "What'd he lose?"

Ugo stood up, slowly. The weariness was back. "What we've all lost, my friend." He looked at the sergeant. "Viva la Chicago!" he said, sadly.

14

Now he was running. He must not stop running. He had to find her. There was a fog in the streets and there were no lights and the Via Flaminia lay wet and cold and dark. There were two possible directions she could have gone: toward the river, or toward the Piazza del Popolo and the city. He hesitated. He could not decide. The bridges and the river were closer than the city. Then he began to run again.

"Lisa!" he shouted.

He ran toward the city. She must be somewhere there, where the tracks of the trolley ran under the archways of the old gate.

The people who were awake or out could see him running. The men playing cards in the wineshops. The drivers waiting beside their horse-drawn carriages for a fare. The women who kept their appointments in the dark side streets.

But it was only a soldier running.

He wore no coat. He was bareheaded.

He was probably drunk. Or he had been robbed. Or he had committed a crime.

They disregarded him.

When he shouted "Lisa!" into the fog and the darkness, they shrugged their shoulders and said, "Eh, the soldati . . . the trouble is always with women."

While he ran.

About the Author

Poet, screenwriter, and novelist, Alfred Hayes, was one of the most important American writers of the 1950s and 1960s. Twice nominated for Academy Awards, he wrote films for Fellini, De Sica (*The Bicycle Thief*), Rossellini (*Paisan*), Zinnemann, and Fritz Lang (*Clash By Night*). His novels include *In Love* and *My Face for the World to See*, and his poem *Joe Hill* was set to music by Earl Robinson and made famous by Joan Baez. Hayes died in 1985.

About Europa Editions

"To insist that if work is good, no matter what, people will read it? Crazy! But perhaps that's why I like Europa . . . They believe in what they are doing above everything. Viva Europa Editions!"
—ALICE SEBOLD, author of *The Lovely Bones*

"A new and, on first evidence, excellent source for European fiction for English-speaking readers."—JANET MASLIN, *The New York Times*

"Europa Editions has its first indie bestseller, Elena Ferrante's *The Days of Abandonment*."—*Publishers Weekly*

"We certainly like what we've seen so far."—*The Complete Review*

"A distinctly different brand of literary pleasure, thoughtfulness and, yes, even entertainment."—*The Ruminator*

"You could consider Europa Editions, the sprightly new publishing venture [...] based in New York, as a kind of book club for Americans who thirst after exciting foreign fiction."—*LA Weekly*

"Europa Editions invites English-speaking readers to 'experience all the color, the exuberance, the violence, the sounds and smells of the Mediterranean,' with an intriguing selection of the crème de la crème of continental noir."—*Murder by the Bye*

"Readers with a taste—even a need—for an occasional inky cup of bitter honesty should lap up *The Goodbye Kiss* . . . the first book of Carlotto's to be published in the United States by the increasingly impressive new Europa Editions"—*Chicago Tribune*

www.europaeditions.com

www.europaeditions.com

AVAILABLE NOW FROM EUROPA EDITIONS

The Jasmine Isle
Ioanna Karystiani
Fiction - 176 pp - $14.95 - isbn 1-933372-10-9

A modern love story with the force of an ancient Greek tragedy. Set on the spectacular Cycladic island of Andros, *The Jasmine Isle*, one of the finest literary achievements in contemporary Greek literature, recounts the story of the old sea wolf, Spyros Maltambès, and the beautiful Orsa Saltaferos, sentenced to marry a man she doesn't love and to watch while the man she does love is wed to another.

I Loved You for Your Voice
Sélim Nassib
Fiction - 256 pp - $14.95 - isbn 1-933372-07-9

"Om Kalthoum is great. She really is."—BOB DYLAN

Love, desire, and song set against the colorful backdrop of modern Egypt. The story of Egypt's greatest and most popular singer, Om Kalthoum, told through the eyes of the poet Ahmad Rami, who wrote her lyrics and loved her in vain all his life. This passionate tale of love and longing provides a key to understanding the soul, the aspirations and the disappointments of the Arab world.

www.europaeditions.com

The Days of Abandonment
Elena Ferrante
Fiction - 192 pp - $14.95 - isbn 1-933372-00-1

"Stunning . . . The raging, torrential voice of the author is something rare."
—JANET MASLIN, *The New York Times*

"I could not put this novel down. Elena Ferrante will blow you away."
—ALICE SEBOLD, author of *The Lovely Bones*

The gripping story of a woman's descent into devastating emptiness after being abandoned by her husband with two young children to care for.

Troubling Love
Elena Ferrante
Fiction - 144 pp - $14.95 - isbn 1-933372-16-8

"In tactile, beautifully restrained prose, Ferrante makes the domestic violence that tore [the protagonist's] household apart evident."—*Publishers Weekly*

"Ferrante has written the 'Great Neapolitan Novel.'"—*Il Corriere della Sera*

Delia's voyage of discovery through the chaotic streets and claustrophobic sitting rooms of contemporary Naples in search of the truth about her mother's untimely death.

www.europaeditions.com

Cooking with Fernet Branca
James Hamilton-Paterson
Fiction - 288 pp - $14.95 - isbn 1-933372-01-X

"A work of comic genius."—*The Independent*

Gerald Samper, an effete English snob, has his own private hilltop
in Tuscany where he wiles away his time working as a ghostwriter
for celebrities and inventing wholly original culinary concoctions.
Gerald's idyll is shattered by the arrival of Marta, on the run from
a crime-riddled former Soviet republic. A series of hilarious
misunderstandings brings this odd couple into ever closer and
more disastrous proximity.

Old Filth
Jane Gardam
Fiction - 256 pp - $14.95 - isbn 1-933372-13-3

"Jane Gardam's beautiful, vivid and defiantly funny novel is a
must."—*The Times*

Sir Edward Feathers has progressed from struggling young barrister
to wealthy expatriate lawyer to distinguished retired judge, living
out his last days in comfortable seclusion in Dorset. The engrossing
and moving account of his life, from birth in colonial Malaya, to
Wales, where he is sent as a "Raj orphan," to Oxford, his career
and marriage, parallels much of the 20th century's dramatic history.

Total Chaos
Jean-Claude Izzo
Fiction/Noir - 256 pp - $14.95 - isbn 1-933372-04-4

"Caught between pride and crime, racism and fraternity, tragedy and light, messy urbanization and generous beauty, the city for Montale is a Utopia, an ultimate port of call for exiles. There, he is torn between fatalism and revolt, despair and sensualism."
—*The Economist*

This first installment in the legendary *Marseilles Trilogy* sees Fabio Montale turning his back on a police force marred by corruption and racism and taking the fight against the Mafia into his own hands.

Chourmo
Jean-Claude Izzo
Fiction/Noir - 256 pp - $14.95 - isbn 1-933372-17-6

"Like the best noir writers—and he is among the best—Izzo not only has a keen eye for detail but also digs deep into what makes men weep."—*Time Out, New York*

Montale is dragged back into the mean streets of a violent, crime-infested Marseilles after the disappearance of his long lost cousin's young son.

www.europaeditions.com

The Goodbye Kiss
Massimo Carlotto
Fiction/Noir - 192 pp - $14.95 - isbn 1-933372-05-2

"The best living Italian crime writer."—*Il Manifesto*

An unscrupulous womanizer, as devoid of morals now as he once was full of idealistic fervor, returns to Italy where he is wanted for a series of crimes. To avoid prison he sells out his old friends, turns his back on his former ideals, and cuts deals with crooked cops. To earn himself the guise of respectability he is willing to go even further, maybe even as far as murder.

Death's Dark Abyss
Massimo Carlotto
Fiction/Noir - 192 pp - $14.95 - isbn 1-933372-18-4

"A narrative voice that in Lawrence Venuti's translation is cold and heartless—but, in a creepy way, fascinating."—*The New York Times*

A riveting drama of guilt, revenge, and justice, Massimo Carlotto's *Death's Dark Abyss* tells the story of two men and the savage crime that binds them. During a robbery, Raffaello Beggiato takes a young woman and her child hostage and later murders them. Beggiato is arrested, tried, and sentenced to life. The victims' father and husband, Silvano, plunges into a deepening abyss until the day the murderer seeks his pardon and Silvano begins to plot his revenge.

www.europaeditions.com

Hangover Square
Patrick Hamilton
Fiction/Noir - 280 pp - $14.95 - isbn 1-933372-06-0

"Hamilton is a sort of urban Thomas Hardy: always a pleasure to read, and as social historian he is unparalleled."—NICK HORNBY

Adrift in the grimy pubs of London at the outbreak of World War II, George Harvey Bone is hopelessly infatuated with Netta, a cold, contemptuous small-time actress. George also suffers from occasional blackouts. During these moments one thing is horribly clear: he must murder Netta.

Boot Tracks
Matthew F. Jones
Fiction/Noir - 208 pp - $14.95 - isbn 1-933372-11-7

"Mr. Jones has created a powerful blend of love and violence, of the grotesque and the tender."
—*The New York Times*

A commanding, stylishly written novel that tells the harrowing story of an assassination gone terribly wrong and the man and woman who are taking their last chance to find a safe place in a hostile world.

www.europaeditions.com

Love Burns
Edna Mazya
Fiction/Noir - 192 pp - $14.95 - isbn 1-933372-08-7

"Starts out as a psychological drama and becomes a strange, funny, unexpected hybrid: a farce thriller. A great book."—*Ma'ariv*

Ilan, a middle-aged professor of astrophysics, discovers that his young wife is having an affair. Terrified of losing her, he decides to confront her lover instead. Their meeting ends in the latter's murder—the unlikely murder weapon being Ilan's pipe—and in desperation, Ilan disposes of the body in the fresh grave of his kindergarten teacher. But when the body is discovered, the mayhem begins.

Departure Lounge
Chad Taylor
Fiction/Noir - 176 pp - $14.95 - isbn 1-933372-09-5

"Entropy noir . . . The hypnotic pull lies in the zigzag dance of its forlorn characters, casting a murky, uneasy sense of doom."
—*The Guardian*

A young woman mysteriously disappears. The lives of those she has left behind—family, acquaintances, and strangers intrigued by her disappearance—intersect to form a captivating latticework of coincidences and surprising twists of fate. Urban noir at its stylish and intelligent best.

www.europaeditions.com

Minotaur
Benjamin Tammuz
Fiction/Noir - 192 pp - $14.95 - isbn 1-933372-02-8

"A novel about the expectations and compromises that humans create for themselves . . . Very much in the manner of William Faulkner and Lawrence Durrell."—*The New York Times*

An Israeli secret agent falls hopelessly in love with a young English girl. Using his network of contacts and his professional expertise, he takes control of her life without ever revealing his identity. *Minotaur* is a complex and utterly original story about a solitary man driven from one side of Europe to the other by his obsession.

Dog Day
Alicia Giménez-Bartlett
Fiction/Noir - 208 pp - $14.95 - isbn 1-933372-14-1

"Giménez-Bartlett has discovered a world full of dark corners and hidden elements."—*ABC*

In this hardboiled fiction for dog lovers and lovers of dog mysteries, detective Petra Delicado and her maladroit sidekick, Garzon, investigate the murder of a tramp whose only friend is a mongrel dog named Freaky. One murder leads to another and Delicado finds herself involved in the sordid, dangerous world of fight dogs. *Dog Day* is first-rate entertainment.

The Big Question
Wolf Erlbruch
Children's Illustrated Fiction - 52 pp - $14.95 - isbn 1-933372-03-6

Named Best Book at the 2004 Children's Book Fair in Bologna.

A stunningly beautiful and poetic illustrated book for children that poses the biggest of all big questions: why am I here? A chorus of voices—including the cat's, the baker's, the pilot's and the soldier's—offers us some answers. But nothing is certain, except that as we grow each one of us will pose the question differently and be privy to different answers.

The Butterfly Workshop
Wolf Erlbruch
Children's Illustrated Fiction - 40 pp - $14.95 - isbn 1-933372-12-5

For children and adults alike: Odair, one of the "Designers of All Things" and grandson of the esteemed inventor of the rainbow, has been banished to the insect laboratory as punishment for his overactive imagination. But he still dreams of one day creating a cross between a bird and a flower. Then, after a helpful chat with a dog . . .

www.europaeditions.com

Carte Blanche
Carlo Lucarelli
Fiction/Noir - 120 pp - $14.95 - isbn 1-933372-15-X

"Carlo Lucarelli is the great promise of Italian crime writing."
—*La Stampa*

April 1945, Italy. Commissario De Luca is heading up a dangerous investigation into the private lives of the rich and powerful during the frantic final days of the fascist republic. The hierarchy has guaranteed De Luca their full cooperation, so long as he arrests the "right" suspect. The house of cards built by Mussolini in the last months of World War II is collapsing and De Luca faces a world mired in sadistic sex, dirty money, drugs and murder.